A
WASH OF
BLACK

CHRIS MCDONALD

RED DOG
UK

CRITICAL ACCLAIM FOR

A WASH OF BLACK

"Wow! Chris McDonald has written a **clever, chilling and absolutely addictive** debut novel with A Wash of Black! A pacy read that will keep you turning the pages. I already want the next book in the DI Erika Piper series…like yesterday!"
—Noelle Holten, author of *Dead Inside*

"An **addictive, gripping read** that pulls you in and has you hooked."

—Sarah Jones, Lost in the Land of Books blog

"I have found my new series obsession. McDonald creates **a strong, rounded lead** in DI Erika Piper and I, for one, cannot wait to read the next."
—M.Sean Coleman, author of *The Code* and
The Cuckoo Wood

Published by RED DOG PRESS 2020

ISBN 978-1-913331-21-4

www.reddogpress.co.uk

For Sarah

For giving me everything I've ever wanted

For Emma and Sophie

Thank you for being my guiding lights

'A painter should begin every canvas with **a wash of black**, because all things in nature are dark except where exposed by the light.'

— Leonardo DaVinci

PROLOGUE

HE WIPES HIS BROW and takes a moment to admire his handiwork - *this is how it should have been done the first time around,* he thinks to himself. It takes all the willpower in the world to step away from the body, the intoxicating aroma of the blood attempting to entice him back, but he knows that he must make sure it has been done properly.

He unfolds the page containing the words he has read countless times; words he could recite in his sleep, but he knows that now is not the time to become careless. He pores over the torn-out page from his favourite book, glancing up every now and then at the scene in front of him. When he is fully happy that nothing has been overlooked, he slips the page back into the plastic wallet and hides it away before making his way carefully off the ice and onto terra firma.

Before he slips out the side door and onto the deserted street, his eyes drink in the bloodbath he is leaving behind. In his head, this isn't murder; it's art.

1

THE FLASHING BLUE LIGHT disturbs the stillness of the morning, dancing over the nearby buildings. There are already three patrol cars and a fleet of vans belonging to the forensic team assembled in the car park. *It must be bad,* I think.

Exiting my own car, I pull my hood as far over my face as I can, to shelter from the howling wind and the unrelenting rain; not out of place on this dismal December morning.

Uniformed police officers scurry about, securing the crime scene with blue and white tape as a few early morning passers-by look on. I duck under and enter the erected blue tent, signing the log book. Looking up, I spot Liam at the door to the ice rink; he's waiting for me, already dressed in a protective suit. I slip into my own suit and pull on a pair of gloves.

'Morning, Erika,' Liam calls, checking his watch, 'Good of you to make it.'

Detective Liam Sutton has been my partner for two years now, three if you count my enforced year of absence. Liam and I gelled quickly and became a hell of a force.

He's tall and lean with clear blue eyes. His hair is shaved tight to his scalp, through choice, not necessity, his dark stubble the same length. He has a penchant for fashion, his fitted shirts always accessorised with a well-chosen tie. If he could get away with a trilby, he'd try.

'Nice to be back,' I say. 'What have we got?'

'Let's find John, I don't want to spoil his fun, he'd never forgive me,' Liam says, attempting a hug but seemingly thinking better of it mid-way through his approach. It turns into an oafish tap on the shoulder instead and I smile at his awkwardness.

We push the tent flaps aside and enter the lobby of the ice rink. It has a disused look about it, the remnants of popcorn machines and dusty hot dog ovens creating a forlorn scene, like we've stepped into a dystopian future.

Scene-of-crime officers are already studiously going about their job, prowling the area with cameras hanging around their necks.

Liam and I cross the foyer and push open the double doors into the ice rink, a frigid blast of ice biting at the small amount of skin foolish enough to be left exposed.

We walk towards the rink, perch on the barrier between solid floor and ice and survey the scene. A shudder courses through my body which has nothing to do with the cold. I'm used to seeing what the worst of humanity is capable of, but sometimes the sheer brutality of it all takes me by surprise. I realise my hand has subconsciously covered my stomach.

In the middle of the ice lie the remains of a woman. She may have been beautiful once, but no longer in death. Serrated blades hold her long limbs tight to the ice. Her head is angled, as if searching for an impossible escape. A gaping black-hole swirls where her neck once was.

On the other side of the rink, a broken door leading to the street is at the mercy of the wind. Police tape has been rolled across it at waist height, and a uniformed officer has been handed the short straw, tasked with keeping vigil just outside in the pouring rain.

John Kirrane is the forensic pathologist present at the scene; the best the city of Manchester has to offer. He is perhaps the thinnest man I have ever seen, as if his appetite is limited by the grisly nature of his job. Understandable really.

From under his hairnet, tight rings of short ginger hair curl around the legs of his glasses, securing them steadfastly in place. His spindly fingers hold a recorder to his lips and he speaks into it at regular intervals, when he spots something of note. He glances towards us and raises a hand in recognition.

'Erika! Give me two minutes and I'll be with you,' he shouts, his voice echoing around us.

We watch him go about his work before clicking off his recording device and walking over the metal stepping plates towards us.

'Erika, it's fantastic to see you. You're back for good now?'

'Yep, and fit as a fiddle,' I nod.

'I'm so glad,' he beams, 'horrible business.' He shakes his head, clears the emotion away. 'Martin has done all he can on the ice,' he says, looking over my shoulder at the head Scene of Crime officer.

He puts his hand in the air to attract Martin's attention. 'I'll just talk through the body and then she's all yours,' he calls. Martin nods his head and stoops down, unzips his bag and readies his tools. He's a short, squat man with the eyes of an eagle.

'Shall we?' asks John.

Liam and I step carefully onto the metal plates and advance towards the body.

The scene is a mess; so much blood. The crimson liquid has pooled underneath her body where the knives were plunged into her arms and legs. It has seeped slowly across the slick, icy surface from those same wounds.

Unusually, the blood from her jagged throat laceration has all spilled in the same direction. Most of it has crept a little way from her neck, while some has spurted quite a distance across the ice.

The dead woman is wearing blue skinny jeans, a yellow halter neck top and black stiletto boots. A thin gold chain sits mournfully on her chest. On her left hand, she wears an engagement ring with a cluster of diamonds.

'Undoubtedly a homicide,' John states. 'Won't know for certain on cause of death until I get her on the slab, but I'd hedge my bets on exsanguination, blood loss from the throat.'

I lean in for a closer look at the throat.

'You'll notice that the blood from the throat has sprayed in one direction,' he continues. 'Usually, you'd expect to see the blood spatter in an arc.' He moves his hand in a slow semi-circular motion to compound his point.

'Has something stopped her head from moving?' Liam interrupts.

'Someone,' replies John. 'If you look here,' he motions to the left side of her face, 'you'll see a faint soleprint,' replies John.

I close my eyes and picture the scene. The killer pins this poor girl down with the steel blades, stands over her. He lifts his boot and presses it onto the side of her face, pushing it down onto the ice. He cuts her throat and keeps his weight on her cheek, ensuring the blood doesn't spray his way.

John's voice stirs me from my thoughts. 'Her tongue has been cut out too.'

'Could be somewhere in here,' I suggest, looking around the room at the foldable plastic seats facing towards the ice.

'Or, the sick fucker who did this has taken it as some sort of trophy,' says Liam.

I nod. 'John, tell Martin about the tongue. He'll get his team to sweep every inch of this place.' John nods, makes a note.

'Time of death?' asks Liam.

'Hard to tell, the temperature has slowed livor mortis but considering blood lividity I'd say roughly between seven and eight hours ago,' replies John.

'So, we're looking around two this morning,' I mutter, checking my watch.

'It's not the first time she's died like that,' says Liam, suddenly.

John and I look at each other, confused, then back to Liam.

'What do you mean?' I ask.

'You really do not appreciate popular culture, do you? Don't you recognise her?'

'I thought her face looked familiar, but I can't place it. What do you mean about dying the same way twice?'

'It's Anna Symons, the actor. She was in a film where she was killed just like this – knives through the arms and legs, throat cut. Her tongue wasn't removed as far as I can remember, though she was naked in the film, so my attention could've been elsewhere.'

'First of all; you are gross.' He sticks his tongue out at me. 'Secondly, why didn't you lead with this information?' I ask, incredulously.

'Well, John was on a roll and I didn't want to interrupt.'

'Fair play,' I say. 'What was the name of the film?'

'No idea. It came out a few years ago.'

'Odd. So the killer has recreated a scene from a film, but made changes?' I say. 'And if the film came out years ago, why now?'

'Beats me,' Liam declares.

I take out my notebook. I need to find out the name of that film.

'I'll have more details on the body in a few days,' says John. 'They'll be on your desk as soon as I'm done. Erika, it really is lovely to see you back. Take care of yourself.' He gives me a warm smile, before turning and signalling to Martin that the body is ready to be moved.

We carefully make our way off the ice and Martin and his team assume control of the crime scene once more.

'Who found the body?' I ask Liam.

'A Mr. Farrier, he's the manager. He's waiting in his office for us.'

We walk back through the foyer and up the stairs. A uniformed officer is waiting at the top of the stairs, to prevent anyone from leaving or entering. We walk past him and enter the manager's room.

It's a small room with a window overlooking the ice rink, though the blinds have been pulled as far across as they can. Behind a flimsy desk sits a man with a trimmed goatee and short, cropped hair.

'Mr Farrier,' I say, extending my hand.

'Please, call me Tony,' he says, getting up from his seat and giving my hand a limp shake. He's as white as a sheet. He motions to two empty chairs in front of him and we take him up on his unspoken offer.

'Tony, I'm Detective Inspector Erika Piper. This is my partner, Detective Sergeant Liam Sutton. Please can you run us through what happened?'

'Well, I got to work at seven this morning as normal. The ice rink doesn't open until later, but there is so much to do; stocktaking, making sure the ice skates are clean, paired and ready to go and what have you.'

He waves his hand as if he knows his information is boring.

'I usually come up here first but I was drawn to the rink, thought I could hear a banging. When I went in, the light was on which was unusual 'cos I always turn them on last. I saw the door smashing against the frame. Broken into, I thought.'

He wipes sweat from his brow with his forearm. Smacks his dry lips together and takes a sip of water. As he sets it down, the plastic bottle springs back into shape with a crack that makes him jump.

'Sorry, I'm a bit on edge.' He barks an embarrassed laugh. 'Anyway, as I walked towards the door I glanced at the ice and saw... it. Her. I ran up to the office as fast as I could and called the police.'

'Was anyone else here?' I ask.

'No, just me,' he replies.

'Wouldn't an alarm go off, if the door was kicked in?' Liam enquires.

He grimaces. 'A few years ago, yeah. But the people who own the rink stopped paying for that service. They don't give a shit about this place, not anymore. No security, CCTV up the duff. It used to be amazing; multi-screen cinema, soft play for the little ones. Now the only part left open is the rink. Reckon it's on the way out too, along with my job,' he adds, glumly.

'Worked here long?' Liam asks.

'I've given twenty years of my life to this fine establishment. It was state of the art when it opened. I started straight out of school, not got the brains to do much else. Though, I worked my way up to manager so I suppose that's something.'

'Has anything like this happened before?'

'God no,' he says, 'we've had a few break-ins over the years, but nothing like this.'

I change tack.

'Where were you last night?'

'I was at my brother's house. He had a bit of a party. I was sensible though 'cos I knew I had to get up early this morning. Hate working with a hangover.'

'And people could verify this?'

'Absolutely, I was there with my wife. Loads of friends there too.'

'Thank you, Tony, you've been very helpful. Obviously, this place will have to stay closed for the time being. If there is any other information you think of, please let us know.'

He takes my proffered card and we leave his room, walking down the stairs to the foyer again.

'What do you reckon?' I ask Liam.

'Can't see why he'd lie,' offers Liam, 'I'll look into his story and make sure he was where he says he was.'

He scribbles in a notebook before replacing it in his pocket. The doors of the rink open and Martin walks out, holding an evidence bag.

'Found a page from a book on the far side of the room,' he says, holding the bag aloft for me to see the contents. 'It seems to be from a crime book, detailing this murder.'

'Good work, Martin. I'd like a copy of the page on my desk as soon as you can.'

'Right-o' he says, already marching towards the door.

'Any sign of the tongue?' Liam calls after him. He stops where he is and turns to face us again, the look on his face suggests he thinks we are wasting his precious time.

'Don't you think I would've mentioned that?' he asks, sarcasm dripping from every syllable. 'No, I think the tongue has gone with whoever has done this.'

He turns around once more and leaves the building.

'I think we're done here,' I say to Liam. 'The SOCO's will let us know if anything else turns up.'

Liam nods in agreement. 'Aren't you glad you picked today to come back to work?'

'Delighted,' I mumble.

2

WE GET IN THE CAR, and Liam and I drive back to the police station in Manchester. The rush hour traffic has just about cleared and we make good time.

It's a quiet journey, both of us lost in our own thoughts about what we've just witnessed. As well as thinking about the case, I'm worried about being back at work.

Coming back after a few weeks off is difficult, but coming back nearly a year after the attack that almost killed me is something else. The question that has whirred round my mind for months comes, once again, to the fore: *Will I still be the same detective I was?*

We enter the police station car park and I pull into my space. The state-of-the-art glass structure looms in front of me, all straight lines, exposed metal work and open, airy spaces. I spot my office on the far end of the third floor and hesitate as I reach for the door handle.

'You OK?' asks Liam.

I nod. 'I will be, it just feels like a big deal, you know?'

He gives my shoulder a squeeze. 'I'll head in and get the room set up for briefing, take your time.'

My eyes fill with tears; this isn't like me.

'Don't go fucking soft on me,' he adds, smiling, and I can't help but laugh as he exits the car and walks towards the sliding doors into the station. I give myself a pep talk, take a few calming breaths and follow suit.

As I enter through the doors, a sense of familiarity washes over me. The front desk is currently being manned by Stuart, a middle-aged man with greying hair and a growing gut. He gives me a warm smile which I reciprocate.

I walk over to the wall of lifts and press the button, which lights up and immediately opens the lift on the far left. I check myself in the mirror which is steeped in unflattering light, wiping away some mascara that has stained the area under my eyes as I rise to the third floor.

When the doors re-open, I leave the lift and walk across the newly carpeted floor. My appearance back at work is met with a solid wall of indifference, which I am very pleased about. The tapping of fingers on computer keyboards and ringing telephones are the sounds of my welcome back.

I pass between the partitioned desks to my office on the other side of the room. Opening the door, I spend a moment taking it all in. It's almost exactly as I'd left it. The case board has been cleared, ready for new photographs and evidence to morbidly decorate it. I've had a new computer installed too.

I sit down on the padded swivel chair and breathe a sigh of relief, searching for the button to turn the computer on, eventually finding it on the back of the console. The computer hums to life and I set about making the briefing PowerPoint.

A short while later, there's a knock on the door.

'Come in,' I call.

Detective Thomas Calder opens the door and sits down. He's changed in the time I've been away. The first thing I notice is his moustache; thick and curled at the end which wouldn't look out of place on Shoreditch High Street. His hair has changed too, longer on top and shaved on the sides. His clothes, as always, are well put together; matching shirt and tie. Slim fit suit. He sets a coffee down on my desk and slides it in my direction.

'Good to see you E. No milk, just how you like it.'

I put my hands on the coffee cup and feel the heat spread through my body. 'Thanks, Tom. Just what I needed. How have things been?'

'Ah, you know, same old same old,' he smiles. 'Not been the same without you though.'

'It's good to be back. What a doozy to return to, eh?' I motion at his face, 'Moustache looks good, bit trendy for Manchester, isn't it?' I say, jokingly.

He pulls a mock offended face.

'And don't think about going any further,' I continue. 'Man-buns are not permitted in this office.'

He laughs, his brown eyes twinkling.

'Maybe this place was better without you after all!'

'Ouch.' Now it's my turn to look playfully hurt. 'Shall we head to briefing and I can fill you in?'

He nods and we walk towards the briefing room. It's a small room at the back of the station with blue plastic chairs arranged in a line, facing towards a pull-down projector screen. A laptop is attached to a projector that's years old and whirrs loudly when in use.

Detective Angela Poynter is sitting at the desk, eyes scanning the laptop screen. She glances up when we enter and gives me a small wave.

She is our technological expert, incredible with computers but socially, a little awkward. Part of me wonders if she's even noticed that I've been off. Angela's appearance has remained, unlike Tom's, absolutely unchanged. Dirty blonde hair is scraped back into a messy ponytail; thick framed glasses perched on her nose. Her green blouse is paired with black combats and black boots; her chosen uniform. Functional, if not overly fashionable.

I move to the front of the room, my heart pounding, like it's my first time leading a briefing. I take a breath, clear my throat and address the team.

'First of all, hi everyone, it's good to be back. Thank you for the flowers you sent me in hospital, they were much appreciated.'

Tom gives me a thumbs up and I can see Angela's eyes drawn to my abdomen.

'OK,' I say, turning to the projector screen. 'Onto the task at hand. Bob is the Senior Investigating Officer on this one, but I've had an email to say he's having some sort of family emergency this morning. He should be in shortly.'

I take another calming breath.

'This morning, at just before seven, we were called to The Ice Bowl in Altrincham. The manager there, Tony Farrier, found the victim, deceased; presumed murdered. Martin hasn't been able to recover anything from the killer yet, no prints, too early for DNA. No CCTV at the rink either. We believe the side door was used to enter and leave; it was hanging off one of its hinges.'

I press a button on the laptop and a picture of Anna Symons, alive and well, appears on the screen. It's a picture lifted from the internet of the actor at a recent awards ceremony. Her hair is intricately set; her subtle make up amplifies her chiselled jawline and feline eyes. She wears a backless red dress with gold high heels. She peers over her shoulder in the way only famous people can get away with.

'Our victim,' I motion to the screen, 'is the actor Anna Symons. Obviously, this is going to kick up a major shit-storm in the media so we need to start making inroads before I call a press conference. News is going to get out, so we want to look like we are on top of this. Angela, can you get us a bit of background on her?'

Angela nods, scribbling in her notebook. I click again and an image of the crime scene appears.

'Jesus,' mutters Tom.

'It's pretty brutal,' I agree. 'Anna Symons had her limbs held to the ice by these,' I indicate the blades with the laser pointer. 'When secured, her throat was cut. Her head was held to one side and her tongue was cut out. John is sending over a picture of the shoe print on her face, if we could analyse that, it may help us. Size, manufacturer of shoe or any distinguishing marks. There was a page from a book left too. Martin is checking it over and I'm waiting for a copy to be sent across.'

'Didn't she die like that in *Blood Ice*?' interjects Angela.

'*Blood Ice*, that's it,' says Liam. 'What a dreadful name for a film.'

'Yeah, I can't remember much about it, except that the deaths were all a bit gruesome,' says Angela. 'I'll find out everything about her that I can.'

'Thanks Angela. Tom, can you arrange for someone to notify her family? She was wearing an engagement ring, so any information about her significant other would be useful. I'd quite like to break the news to him myself; see if we can get him in, gauge his reaction.'

'On it,' he nods.

'Right, that's it for now, let's get to it. Liam, my office please. Let's go through what we've seen this morning, see if there are any pieces we can make fall into place.'

Half an hour later, Angela and Tom's heads appear on either side of the door frame.

'Wow, 10 out of 10 for synchronicity,' I chuckle, holding up an imaginary judge's paddle.

Tom pumps his fist and cheers, 'Angela, you said it would be a waste, but all those months of practice have paid off,' he laughs.

'Boss,' says Angela, ignoring his frivolity. 'Good news. Anna Symons was in a bar in Altrincham last night called Limas. A woman posted a photo on Twitter posing with Symons, saying how she couldn't believe she'd met her. It was posted at 11:57pm which is only a few hours before the approximate time of death. I've got the CCTV footage from the street outside the bar. I've had a quick look and she leaves with two others, both men. She looks like she's had a bit too much to drink, stumbling about and having to be held up. I'll send it across to you now.'

Without another word, she backs out of the doorway and marches towards her desk.

'Great work,' I call after her. I turn to Tom. 'What have you got?'

'Well, I've arranged for a couple of uniforms to go to her mother's house to notify her of Anna's death. She lives in Altrincham, not far from the bar, actually. They should be there soon. As for her fiancé, he's called Rory Knox. He works for a company in London but he's been away on business this week. They gave me his number and I managed to get in touch with him. He was driving back from Bradford, poor bastard.'

'What's wrong with Bradford?' I joke.

Tom and Liam both laugh.

'I haven't told him anything except that we need to speak to him; he's on his way here. Should arrive within the hour.'

'Thanks Tom, top notch. Please can you prep the interview room?'

3

THE LIFT DOORS SLIDE open and a tall man – well over six foot – wearing a white shirt, pink pinstripe tie and a three-piece charcoal grey suit walks out. His hair is dark, slicked back with a generous helping of gel.

The soles of his patent leather shoes squeak as he approaches the nearest desk. He oozes sophistication. He exchanges a few words with Liam who nods, gets up and accompanies him to my door.

'Erika,' he says, leading the man into the room, 'this is Mr. Knox.'

'Please, call me Rory,' he says, scratching his neck nervously. 'Forgive me for being blunt, but why am I here?'

'Rory, I'm Detective Inspector Erika Piper and I'm afraid I've got some bad news. Please take a seat.'

Liam sits down on my side of the desk. Rory sits down on the other. I take a breath.

'This morning, we found the body of Anna Symons. We have reason to believe that she was murdered.'

The skin on his forehead creases as he frowns.

'Anna? Murdered? No, you must have the wrong person,' he says, shaking his head. 'I spoke to her last night, she was fine. She was just about to curl up on the sofa with a book. It can't be her.'

'I know it's a lot to take in,' I reply, 'but we are certain that the body is Anna's. I'm sorry.'

Rory sits forward in his chair, his head falling into his hands. Strands of hair break loose from behind his ears. His world as he's known it has ended; everything will be different from this point on. He glances up after a minute.

'How?' he croaks.

'Are you sure you want to know the details?'

'Tell me.' It's almost a growl.

'She was found at The Ice Bowl in Altrincham, the autopsy is not back yet so we can't be 100% certain, but we believe she died from blood loss from a laceration to the throat.'

'Like in *Blood Ice*?' he asks, his head snapping up to look at me, eyes wide.

'We believe there may be similarities between the two deaths, yes.' I decide to spare him the extraneous details, though I know he is picturing the scene from the film in his mind's eye. He begins to slump forwards in his chair and lowers his head to look at the floor, the reality of it all seeping in to his bones.

'Have you found who did it?' he whispers.

'Not yet,' I admit to the top of his head, 'but we're working on it. Please take as much time as you need to get your head around it. When you are feeling up to it, would you mind answering some questions? It would help us with our investigation.'

He nods again.

'Can I have a few minutes alone please?' he asks. 'Then I'll answer any questions, I'll do anything I can to help.'

'Of course,' I reply. 'Stay here, as long as you need. We'll be outside when you are ready.'

THE RADIATOR IN THE interview room has been left on too long. I can feel beads of sweat form on my scalp and make their way down my forehead. The room is small, almost oppressively so; sometimes a useful psychological tool during interrogations with savvy, tight-lipped criminals. There is no clock, no window; no way to judge the passing of time. A low table, currently holding 3 plastic cups of water, separates Rory from Liam and me.

'Thanks for doing this Rory; anything you can tell us could be useful in helping to catch the responsible party. We're going to record this, standard procedure,' I say, noticing his eyes dart to the camera in the corner of the interview room. 'If you want to stop at any stage, please say so. Remember, you are here voluntarily.'

Without looking at us, he nods, his glassy eyes fixed on a point on the table. His shoulders rise and fall in a steady rhythm, like his body is on autopilot. His suit jacket is draped over the back of his chair and a tuft of hair is showing over the top of his open collared shirt. He looks like he has aged ten years in the past hour.

'Commencing interview with Rory Knox. Present are Detective Sergeant Liam Sutton and Detective Inspector Erika Piper. Interview conducted at,' Liam pulls up his shirt sleeve to check his watch, '13:33 on Saturday the first of December 2019. Rory Knox has declined the offer of legal representation. He is here of his own free will.' Liam gives him a reassuring nod. 'Rory, please can you tell us about your relationship with Anna Symons?'

'Yeah… we met, uh,' he looks up, time travelling in his head, 'seven years ago. She was doing some filming in the park near my work. I happened to walk past during my lunch break and saw her mid-scene. I waited in the small crowd that had gathered and watched her; I couldn't take my eyes off her. When the scene ended, our eyes met. There was this instant electricity. I pointed to a nearby bench and she nodded.'

He smiles, a welcome memory amongst the current chaos.

'I didn't think she'd actually come, but eventually she did. We introduced ourselves and talked for a while but I needed to get back to work, I was already late. Took a bollocking for it but it was worth it. We arranged to meet up later that day, when she was done. We met in the city and went for a few drinks. And the rest, as they say, is history.'

I give him a few seconds to bask in the celebration of life.

'Was it always a happy relationship?'

'Mostly, she is… was, so much fun.' He winces at the past tense, takes a few seconds to steady himself. 'She was caring, funny, adventurous. But, I guess, like any relationship, we had our ups and downs. She was away a lot with her job, all over the world for months at a time. She was massively in demand and that was amazing for her career, but it put a strain on us. Long distance is never easy…' he trails off.

I let the silence linger, hoping he'll go on.

'About 5 years ago, she was making *that* film. The director and her got very close… too close… she had an affair. It lasted for a couple of weeks and then she finished it. She told me a few months later.'

'And you forgave her?'

He thinks about this whilst biting his thumb nail. After some deliberation, he says: 'Everyone makes mistakes. It took me a while to get over it, but we got there. From then on, I found it really hard when she went away for work, took me a long time to trust her again.'

'Understandable,' I say. 'Rory, can you think of anyone who would want to harm Anna?'

He ponders the question. 'I really don't. She was extremely likeable.' His shoulders are starting to slouch.

'You're doing so well Rory, just a few more questions and then this will all be over,' I say, giving him an encouraging smile. 'Why was she in Manchester? You lived in London together, didn't you?'

'We did, yes. She was visiting her mother while I was away on business. I was coming in a day early to surprise her. We had planned to spend the rest of the week up here before heading back down south.'

'How long were you away for?'

He puffs out his cheeks and exhales loudly, implying his job is the last thing that matters to him at this moment in time. 'I've been away for six days. Three days in Liverpool and three in Bradford.'

'And what do you do?'

'I work in advertising. Film trailers, TV adverts and what have you.'

'You said earlier that she was on the sofa with a book when you spoke. Do you remember what time that was?'

'I can tell you exactly what time.'

He turns in his chair and fishes his mobile phone from the inside pocket of his jacket. He puts it on the table for us to see, unlocks it and accesses his call list. Her name features a few times on the list, but he points to the one of importance – the one from last night at 20:26. I scribble a note onto the page in front of me.

'And you are sure she definitely didn't mention any other plans?' I ask.

He looks confused at the line of questioning.

'No,' he says, brow furrowed. 'She'd just made a hot chocolate and was about to open a script her agent had sent over when I'd called.'

'Rory, we have CCTV footage of her leaving a bar in Altrincham at around 12:30am. She leaves with two men and appears to be extremely intoxicated. Sorry to have to tell you this,' I say, sincerely.

He looks angry, whether it's at me for breaking this news to him or at Anna for deceiving him, I can't be sure. I push the printed CCTV images in front of him. He glances at them. If he was angry before, he's apoplectic now.

'Is this a fucking joke?' he shouts, pushing himself to standing whilst sending the chair crashing into the wall behind.

'Rory, do you recognise these men?' I say.

'That fucking bitch! I can't believe she'd fucking do this to me.'

He snatches the piece of paper off the desk and looks at it again before slamming it back down on the table. The anger rages in his eyes, he's looking at the photos like he could burn a hole in them. Slowly, rage turns to hurt. He picks the chair up, falls back into it and starts to sob.

'Rory,' I repeat, 'do you know these men?'

He blows his nose on a tissue and takes a sip of water, composing himself.

'Only one of them,' he gets out eventually, his voice now small. 'The taller one is that fucking director she had an affair with. The one who directed *Blood Ice*.'

4

THE WINDSCREEN WIPERS ARE fighting a losing battle against the lashing rain as we crawl along the motorway.

'Shall we stop at the next services?' asks Liam. 'It's getting a bit hard to see what's in front of us.'

'Yeah, I guess so. We're about half way to Conwy anyway. We could grab a coffee and look at what was sent through this morning. What time is it?'

'Just coming up to eleven. Oh, you might be on the news,' he says, adjusting the volume of the radio above the din of the hammering rain.

The fast-paced rock song finishes with the singer's abrasive bark, and the jingle for the news starts.

From the news centre at eleven, my name is Craig Myers. Police have launched a murder investigation after finding the body of British actress, Anna Symons. Her body was found yesterday. No arrests have been made and police are urging members of the public who may have seen Anna in Altrincham on Friday night to get in touch. Anna starred in many Hollywood films, including The Mistress and Blood Ice though she may be best known for portraying Detective Francesca Uro in the long running BBC series Dust. Our thoughts are with Anna's family at this time. Vauxhall say they have made the tough decision…

Liam turns the volume down.

'Not even name checked,' he teases.

'I'm just pleased they didn't use the audio from the presser,' I reply, 'I hate hearing my voice played back. We've had quite a few calls in response to the press conference though, from people in the bar when Anna arrived. From what I've heard, she was sober when she came in and was happy to have pictures with anyone who wanted one. She was in good spirits and had a few drinks, danced for a while. Apparently, she became intoxicated quite quickly and left with two men; one of whom has been confirmed as Reuben Amado, the director of *Blood Ice*.'

Liam absorbs the information.

'You think she was drugged?'

'It's plausible. She was there for just over an hour, and some of that time was spent taking photos. We'll know more once John has the toxicology report back.'

'Did she come on her own?' he asks.

'No, apparently she arrived with another female.'

'But you think she came to meet Amado?'

I've been turning this question over in my head since Rory's revelation yesterday.

'Possibly, it makes sense. Especially since she told her fiancé that she was having an evening on the sofa. She'd definitely want to keep that meeting a secret. We'll see what we can get out of him later; hopefully he doesn't mind us turning up on set.'

I indicate into the left-hand lane, having spotted the sign for the services. I follow the curve of the junction into the car park, avoiding deep potholes, and get as close to the door as possible. We run into the foyer with our coats pulled over our heads and Liam points to the coffee shop.

'Get me a cappuccino, would you? I'm dying for a piss,' he says.

'Charming,' I reply, as he rushes off in the direction of the toilet.

I approach the counter and order two coffees, eyeing up a chocolate muffin but deciding against it. I think of the level of fitness I'd had before the incident almost a year ago, and the hours spent in the gym trying to claw it back so I move away from the cake display and the temptation of the sugary treat. Not that I didn't enjoy binge eating in front of the TV after leaving hospital.

A few minutes later, my name is called. I collect the coffees, the name scrawled on mine spelled incorrectly, and find a table near the window. Liam ambles through the seats, glancing left and right looking for me.

'Better?' I ask, as he sits down.

'Yep,' he says, taking a sip of the coffee, 'cheers for this.'

He sets the cup down and looks at the photocopied page I've put on the table.

'Is that what Martin sent across?'

'It is indeed. As expected, nothing left on the page from the killer, but obviously he wanted us to see it for some reason. Have a look.'

He takes the page and reads it aloud.

Her body writhed as he plunged the final knife into her thigh. She was pinned down; blood soaking through her clothes and spreading across the ice. It was mesmerising. It was art.

'Why are you doing this?' she whimpered with the last ounce of energy left in her.

'You know why,' he replied.

She shook her head but he didn't say anymore. Instead, he picked up the machete and approached her. He kicked her head to one side and pushed down on her cheek with his boot; she tried to fight it but didn't have nearly enough energy left. Without another word, he sliced her throat from one side to the other. He'd done his research; he'd known there'd be a lot of blood but the amount spraying from her throat was still a pleasant surprise.

He waited for a while, mesmerised, until the blood flow slowed before checking her pulse. She was still alive, just. He grabbed her hair and pulled her head up so that he could look in her eyes one last time. Pushing her chin down roughly, he took hold of her tongue, his hands slipping on a mix of saliva and blood. He took the machete once more and cut it out. He put it in a clear, zipped bag and stuffed it in the front of his backpack. He took one more look at her as the life ebbed away from her body and then he left. She'd brought this on herself. Now he could stop. But would he?

'Jesus,' Liam says. 'Grim. So this is the source material for Anna's murder?'

'It would seem so. It's from a book called *The Threat* by E. F. Bennett. It did tremendously well for a debut novel and the film rights were sold almost straight away. *The Threat* became *Blood Ice*. Two more books were released in *The Threat* series; *The Violent Threat* and *The Final Threat.*'

'Which means, if the killer is using these books as a blueprint, we could potentially have 2 more murders?'

'That's assuming he only picks one death from each book.'

Liam lowers his gaze to the page again. He holds it up for me to look at.

'Why do you reckon he has highlighted *through her clothes*?' he asks.

I point at the other words on the page that have been singled out. '*Tongue* and *cut it out* have been highlighted too. At first I wasn't sure but then I thought about what you said about the film.'

'That she was naked?'

'That, yes, and also that her tongue wasn't cut out. I think the highlighted sections are the differences between the film and the book, and therefore the film and the real-life murder.'

He scans the page again and seems to agree with my hypothesis.

'Why would he leave this at the crime scene?' he wonders aloud, but more to himself.

I shrug my shoulders and take a sip of the coffee. The warmth seeps down my throat and spreads through my body.

'Do you think the killer is one of those geeks who watches a film with a notebook and logs inaccuracies on the internet?'

Liam takes out his phone and taps the screen a few times. He raises his shoulders and tilts his head, adopts a nerdy voice; 'Ah, during the 1972 New Year's Eve celebrations, Forrest Gump drinks a Dr. Pepper with a logo that wasn't devised until the mid-1980s.'

He pushes imaginary glasses up his nose to emphasise the point.

'Someone actually wrote that on the internet?'

'Yeah, clearly a psychopath,' he laughs.

Glancing outside, I notice that the rain has relented somewhat and suggest getting back on the road. Liam nods his agreement and we return to the car, coffees in hand.

'It's about 45 minutes from here to Conwy,' I say, as I restart the sat nav.

Liam rummages through the glovebox and picks up a CD case, the only one in the car. 'Shall we see how rusty we are?' he asks.

As well as discussing whatever case we happen to be on, Liam and I have spent countless hours of travelling trying to nail every harmony the four beautiful Swedes committed to record on ABBA Gold.

'Get it in,' I reply.

WE ARRIVE IN CONWY with slightly raspy throats. Golden threads of sunlight are fighting to break through the clouds, illuminating the still water in the harbour. The medieval castle looms on the skyline, climbing as if to touch the heavens. It's an impressive greeting from the small coastal town.

I indicate into the castle's car park and stop by the security cordon. A portly security guard in high-vis waddles towards our unmarked police car. I lower my window and treat him to a smile.

'Castle's shut today love, sorry,' he says, bending down to look in at us. 'They're filming a movie up there.'

'That's why we're here,' I reply, flashing my police ID, 'the director is expecting us.'

I watch as he pulls his radio up to his mouth and mumbles into it. A moment later, an indecipherable garble emits from the walkie-talkie, though he seems to have understood it because he moves a few of the cones that were blocking our way and waves us through.

I put the car into first gear and rev up the hill towards the spaces. Most of them have been taken up by huge production trucks and trailers so I pull into one of the spaces at the far end of the car park.

We show our passes to the security guards who stop us momentarily, before letting us past with slightly quizzical looks. The large courtyard of the castle buzzes with activity. Blinding lights heat the enclosed space and people with lanyards and clipboards run to and fro, avoiding the camera tracks laid out precisely on the floor.

A few actors are sitting around on chairs, noses stuck into scripts, poring over their lines; others are having their make-up reapplied whilst glued to their mobile phones. A number of intense conversations go on around the castle's open square.

'Places!' screams a man suddenly, making me jump. People spring into action. A cameraman takes his position behind his equipment; his eye presses against the viewfinder and his hands adjust knobs on the side of his gear. Actors rise from their seats and take their place in the foreground, centre stage. The main guy who I vaguely recognise from something on TV is speaking to the man we're here to see; Reuben Amado.

If I was asked to draw a hipster, I'd draw Reuben. Lank, shoulder-length hair emerges from under a woollen beanie hat and a long beard spills down onto a blue and white plaid shirt.

Tight black jeans torn at the knees and a pair of maroon Doc Martins complete his bohemian uniform.

He's taller than when I'd imagined him; maybe pushing 6' 1". He agrees with whatever the actor is saying and points to a spot on the floor, to which the actor moves. A man with a clapperboard steps in front of the camera.

'Action!' shouts Reuben. The actors begin their scene, though it barely has time to get started before he puts a stop to it. 'Come on guys, give me more,' he yells in the general direction of the actors, who move back to their starting positions and begin the scene again. Reuben watches the action, immediately looking agitated. He lets the cameras roll for about a minute before ending it again.

'For fuck's sake!' he screams, pulling off his headphones. 'George, you're about to kill this woman and you're holding her like a fucking antique! Like this!' he roars, marching towards the woman.

Without warning, he grabs her by the throat and shoves her towards the castle wall. She bounces off it roughly with a cry before falling to her knees. She uses her hand to put pressure on the back of her head and when she releases it a moment later, her hand is covered in blood.

'Jesus Christ, Reuben, that fucking hurt!' the woman shouts. She gets to her feet and walks past Reuben off the set in the direction of the car park, presumably towards one of the trailers.

'At least it looked fucking real!' hisses Reuben, throwing his arms up in exasperation. There is a silence that no one seems willing to break. 'Everyone take five,' he shouts, as he walks towards his chair and throws himself into it. Liam and I take this lapse in action as our cue.

We approach Reuben and introduce ourselves, though he looks less than pleased. 'How the fuck did you get on set?' he spits, standing up. With that, he storms off.

'Great first impression,' whispers Liam. As we are about to follow him, a mountain of a man with a scowl on his face advances towards us.

'Who the fuck are you and why the fuck are you on my set?' he shouts in an American accent, pushing Liam on the shoulder and showering him with saliva. Liam pulls out his police badge and shows it to the man.

'I suggest you keep your cool, sunshine,' Liam replies, calmly. 'We're here to see Mr Amaro. As long as everything is in order, he'll be back in no time. What's your name?'

'None of your fucking business,' he growls, before stalking off.

5

I LOOK AROUND REUBEN'S trailer and I am deeply unimpressed. I was expecting plush seats, polished wooden floors and a huge fridge chilling an expensive bottle of Cristal. This is not what Reuben has. His trailer is so cramped that Liam and I are sitting on the caravan-style seats at one end of it whilst he sits on the floor, glaring at us. The plastic covered walls are stained a colour similar to dehydrated urine and it smells like a teenage boy's bedroom.

Two mugs of tea sit on the small, foldaway table and the director is swigging from a bottle of non-alcoholic beer.

'What was all that about?' Liam opens the questioning.

Amaro shrugs nonchalantly, takes a swig from his bottle.

'I need realism. Audiences are smarter than ever, they can sense if something isn't a hundred percent genuine. George is a good actor, but in that scene, he's just found out she's been cheating on him. Did you see him? He was wheeling her round like a fucking collectable. No-one is going to believe that.'

Liam and I cast a sideways glance at each other.

'I was just trying to show everyone what it needed to look like,' Reuben sighs, contemplatively. 'Maybe I went a bit far. I didn't mean to knock her head against the wall, I should have warned her.'

So he's not a *total* monster, I think.

'Mr. Amaro, do you know why we are here?' Liam asks.

This question is met with a snort of derision. 'I might have an inkling. Why did you have to come onto the set though?' he whines. 'You know this is getting out onto social media as we speak. And Jay isn't going to be happy.'

'Jay?' I ask.

'My boss. He's the executive producer, the man with the money. I imagine he will have something to say.' I neglect to tell him that Jay, who is presumably the loud-mouthed American, has indeed already had something to say.

'Look, Reuben, we only care about finding out what happened to Anna. Why don't you tell us about Friday night?'

'Friday night…' he trails off.

His fingers pull at the label on his bottle, creating a little pile of discarded paper on the carpeted floor. I don't take my eyes off him.

'On Friday night,' he says after a prolonged silence. 'My friend Ed and I met in a bar near Manchester for a bit of a business meeting.'

'Odd time for a business meeting,' comments Liam.

'I use business meeting loosely. We have a joint event coming up next week and we were discussing the format. It was the only time we were both free and in the area. Thought we'd do it over a beer.'

'So why did you invite Anna?'

He looks confused. 'Why would I invite her? I haven't spoken to Anna in years, not since…'

'Since your affair?'

'Ha! Hardly an affair,' he snorts. 'We fucked a few times. Her and her boyfriend, I want to say Ryan...' The intonation of his voice rises during the last part of the sentence, making it sound like a question.

'Rory,' I interject.

'That's it,' Reuben says, picking up the story, 'she and Rory were having a hard time and I was having a dry spell. We were on set together and got involved. I didn't feel good about it, but... you've seen her,' he flashes a wide grin, looking at Liam. 'Who's gonna say no to that when she's throwing it at you?'

Liam looks like he's putting in a lot of effort not to comment and a little of Reuben's bluster is lost at Liam's apparent lack of interest.

'Anyway, as soon as filming stopped, we stopped. I haven't seen her since.'

'And the next time you see her just happens to be a few hours before she is murdered.'

It's not a question, but I let the silence linger between us. In my experience, the person I'm talking to is often the one to break it and break it he does.

'I know how it must look,' he mutters.

'How must it look, Mr. Amaro?'

He opens his mouth to reply, then thinks better of it. Maybe he's better at holding a silence than I gave him credit for. Liam tries a different tack.

'So Anna arrives. She hasn't been invited by you, or so you claim.' Amado attempts to interrupt but Liam holds a hand up. 'So what happens next?'

'She arrived at the bar and caused a stir. People were clamouring for a picture with her. I'd assumed when she had come in that it was a coincidence that she was there, but she searched around the bar for us and eventually caught my eye. It's like she came to Limas knowing I was there. Her and her friend made their way over to our table. We hugged and shot the shit for a while, discussed our current projects and whatnot.'

'Was she drunk?'

'Not when she arrived, no. But about an hour after she arrived, suddenly she was out of it. She was falling over and bumping into people on the dance floor so Ed and I decided that the best thing to do was to get her home. We managed to get her off the dance floor and over to the bar to get her some water, then we took her outside. Ed got a bus from just outside the bar and I took her to a hotel just up the street and paid the receptionist. I would've put her in a taxi home but she couldn't tell me her address. Then I walked home.'

'So the receptionist of the hotel could verify this?'

'Well, no,' he says, slowly. 'Actually, now that I think about it, I was going to pay the receptionist but Anna refused to go into the hotel. We argued in front of the building but she wouldn't budge, so I gave her the money and walked away. I assume she went in.'

'So no one can vouch for you?'

'I live alone so no-one can tell you that I got home, but I did,' he shrugs. I scribble in my notebook to try and get the CCTV near the hotel. I also need to check if Ed, whoever he may be, definitely got the bus outside the bar.

'Who is this Ed fella you were meeting?' I ask.

'Ed Bennett, he's an author. He wrote *The Threat* books, you might've heard of them? He and I go way back, we went to university together. When he sold the film rights, he got me the director gig. I'd just won an award at Cannes for a short film, so it was great timing. *Blood Ice* was my first feature length so I owe him! We wrapped on the second in the series too a few months ago, the premiere is in a couple of weeks.'

I can't believe it.

'Let's get this straight,' I say, tersely. 'You and Ed – the writer of *The Threat* – are in a bar in Altrincham discussing business. Ed is the author of a novel containing a particularly grisly murder scene. You directed the movie adaptation with the same murder scene, in which Anna played the victim. Then, on the night you both *happen* to bump into Anna in a bar, she is murdered in the same way.'

Amaro's face visibly pales. I realise that the details of the murder must be a revelation to him. Or perhaps he realises just how bad this looks for him.

He asks to be excused for a few minutes and when we acquiesce, he stands up and walks the few steps to the trailer's door. I follow him and as I take a seat on the top step, I inform him that we have a warrant to search the trailer. He shrugs his shoulders as he pulls out a cigarette and paces to and fro.

To my right, Liam pushes himself out of his seat and walks to the tiny kitchenette area. He tugs a pair of blue gloves out of his pocket and pulls them on.

He opens a few of the drawers, has a quick scan and a poke about before closing them again. He grasps the handle of a cupboard, pulls it open and I crane my neck to get a better view of what he is doing.

Inside the cupboard is a brown wicker basket, which I assume is being used as a washing basket due to the clothes spilling out of it. Liam begins to rifle through the basket, whilst I keep my eye on Reuben.

He has stopped pacing and is now sitting on the ground, the burning stub of the cigarette between his fingers, his eyes following a row of ants that scurry about.

Liam waves his hands in the air to get my attention before unfurling an item of clothing. He holds up a blue boiler suit. It is covered in blood.

'Mr Amaro,' I say.

He looks up from the ground, the dying cigarette smouldering in his mouth.

'You're coming with us.'

6

I STRETCH MY LEGS out as far as they can reach on the sofa and listen to Darren bang around in the kitchen. I've dubbed tonight 'the make-or-break dinner' in my mind and I've been dreading it for a while.

Darren and I have been dating for just under three years now, but it feels like it's been coming to a natural ending for a while now. He's never been a fan of my line of work. He appreciates the importance of the job, but doesn't like that it's me on the frontline – a feeling that has grown even stronger since the incident almost a year ago. In fairness, I can't say I blame him, I'd probably feel the same if the roles were reversed.

I turn onto my side and push my head into the cushion, closing my eyes. My thoughts drift to the moment Darren and I first met. I was admiring a painting of a man from the Victorian era in a quiet wing of the Manchester art gallery when a stranger had sidled up. He had commented on how accurate the artist had been in his rendering and when I enquired if he had known the man depicted in the painting, he pulled a mock-horrified face, claiming that he thought I was the sitter in the portrait.

Despite this feeble attempt at humour, I laughed aloud, much to the chagrin of the other gallery-goers. We then spent the rest of the afternoon strolling around the exhibit admiring the artwork before heading for a drink. At the end of the night, we had swapped numbers and he kissed me, and we had been an item ever since.

I open my eyes and take in the intricate print of the sofa cushion close up. Perhaps I'm being pessimistic about the state of our relationship; just because he doesn't want to hear about my day doesn't mean he doesn't care about my career, does it? Maybe in his head ignorance is bliss.

He is still as caring as he was when we met, though some of his humour has worn off, much more serious these days. I guess that comes with age and growing responsibilities but maybe that's what I miss. I roll over and lift the wine glass off the floor, taking a sip of the crisp white and enjoying the fruity smell which fills my nostrils.

'Dinner is served,' Darren announces from the kitchen. I ease myself off the sofa, carrying my nearly empty glass of wine and follow his voice into the kitchen. Peaceful piano music plays from a speaker on the windowsill and I can feel the tears fighting to escape my eyes when I see the effort he has gone to.

Every surface has been covered with flickering tea-light candles and a beautifully presented meal sits pride of place on the table. Darren walks over to me and kisses my forehead before pulling a chair out for me to sit on. I take my place and pick up my knife and fork.

'Darren, this is amazing,' I say, gazing around the room. He smiles and raises his glass of beer, which I clink with mine. We ease into conversation, chatting about his day and carefully avoiding mentioning mine. We discuss the half marathon we've both entered and laugh at the training, or lack thereof, we've completed so far.

Once we are finished our meals, he excuses himself from the table, taking our empty plates and dumping them into the sink before returning with a chocolate cake which he claims he has baked himself, though the partially crushed box I saw in the recycling bin earlier may suggest otherwise.

As he sets the plate down in front of me, my phone, which I thought was on silent, emits a pulsating dance song from the 80s that indicates an incoming call. Darren casts a glance at the screen and his expression immediately sours. JOHN PATHOLOGIST flashing on the screen is one way to ruin the romantic atmosphere.

'Please tell me you're not actually going to answer it,' he says, as my hand instinctively reaches for the device.

'I have to, sorry, I've been waiting on this all day. I promise I'll be quick,' I reply as I open the kitchen door and step into the back garden. I press the green button and greet John.

'Hi Erika, I'm so sorry for calling you at this time. I know you're not on shift at the minute but I thought you'd like to know my findings on Anna,' opens John.

'Don't be silly John, I'm all ears,' I reply.

'Well, I was right about cause of death; exsanguination. It was the laceration to the throat that did it. The incision was deep and oblique, caused by a non-serrated blade, most likely a meat cleaver or machete. There are no defence injuries so we know she didn't put up a fight. We also did a tox report because of the drunken state you reported she was in. There was a small trace of alcohol present in her blood, but not enough to intoxicate her to that degree. The amount of flunitrazepam in her blood, however, was more than enough to put her in that condition.'

'Flunitrazepam? As in Rohypnol?'

'The very same.'

'So someone has drugged her and then murdered her?'

'Certainly looks that way,' replies John, before pressing on. 'I've taken a number of photos of her face to capture the impressions left behind from the boot. I'm going to send them across to your office. Hopefully you can match them up to a manufacturer. I'll also send across the full post-mortem report. Enjoy the rest of your night.'

I mutter my thanks and reciprocate the farewell. With my phone stashed in my pocket, I push the door handle down and re-enter a very different looking kitchen. The candles have been blown out and only my cake remains on the table. I can hear gunshots and shouting emanating from the TV in the living room, signalling Darren's participation in the evening as complete.

I sigh, pick up my plate and spoon and enter the living room. Darren is sitting upright in the tartan Sherlock chair. He keeps his eyes firmly fixed on the TV as I enter.

I set my cake on the sofa and squeeze in beside him on the chair.

'Sorry Daz, I had to take it. Let's not let it spoil tonight.'

His eyes flicker towards me for a split second and when I nibble on his earlobe, he emits an audible sigh.

'Come upstairs in a few minutes,' I whisper, before pushing myself out of the seat and ascending the thickly carpeted stairs.

I walk into the bedroom and pull out the top drawer. It's mostly filled with everyday underwear, standard comfies. I poke about a bit and unearth what I'm looking for; the lingerie for special occasions. We haven't had sex since before the incident and Darren has been patient, though at times I can tell he is very frustrated.

I pull off my clothes and put on the lacy knickers and matching bra. I look at myself in the mirror, my eyes drawn not to what I'm wearing, but to the glossy scar to the left of my bellybutton. My mind starts to drift towards what happened that night when I hear movement from downstairs so I dim the light and get under the covers.

Darren pushes the door open and enters the weakly lit room. I can see the corners of his mouth spread into a grin as he creeps towards the bed. He pulls the duvet off his side and as he looks me up and down and registers what I'm wearing, he howls like a wolf which makes me laugh. His eyes flick momentarily towards the scar but quickly leave it behind as they lock onto my eyes.

I pull him close and he kisses me hard. His stubble scratches my skin, the slight grazes adding to the sensations coursing through my body. He pushes my head to the side gently and works his way down to my neck. As I close my eyes to focus on the feeling, the darkness transports me to another world.

He's there. In the corner of the room. I hear his uneven breaths before I see him crawling out from his hiding place. His face is obscured by a balaclava but his eyes are locked on me, eyes that burn with calculated rage. He takes one step out of the shadows and as he slowly extends his arm, I see the blade shimmering in his hand. I've never been more aware of my mortality. I implore him to be calm and assure him that I'm here to help him, that I have his best interests at heart. After what seems like an eternity of deliberation, he makes a sudden jolt forward.

'Fuck off!' I scream and push him off me, lashing at his head with my fists. As he rolls away from me, I realise that it is not the man who stabbed me and left me for dead, but rather Darren. He looks hurt.

'Darren, I'm sorry,' I cry. 'I thought you were him, I saw him in the room.'

He moves to the edge of the bed and plants his feet on the floor, shaking his head. In complete silence, he picks up his shirt from the foot of the bed and slides his arms in.

'I can't do this anymore,' he says quietly, whilst fastening the buttons. 'I know what you've been through, and I know it can't be easy to deal with, but I can't do this. You aren't even trying to get past it.'

Once these words have left his mouth, he immediately looks like he wishes he could take them back.

'I am fucking trying to get past it!' I yell. 'Do you think I like the memory of being stabbed hanging over me every day? Do you think I like that he has pretty much taken away my chance...my ability to be a... a mother?' I can barely get the last word out through the tears. I glare at him and he recoils slightly.

'I'm sorry, I didn't mean it to come out like that. I just mean, even before you got stabbed, we weren't happy,' he says quietly. 'It's unfortunate that you can't have...'

'Unfortunate?' I interrupt, not wanting to hear the end of his sentence. 'Unfortunate? Losing your bank card is unfortunate. Dropping your phone down the toilet is unfortunate. Not being able to have children is a fucking tragedy. Get the fuck out.'

He stands up and looks resigned. The beginning of an end hangs silently in the space between us.

'I'll stay at a friend's tonight,' he says. 'We can talk about us in the morning.'

With that, he leaves the room and doesn't look back.

CHARLOTTE RAISES HER DRINK in a toast.

'What a prick!'

We're in a booth in Foragin – the new gin bar in Marple, where we both live. Charlotte has been my best friend since childhood. We've grown up together and experienced everything life has had to throw at us – cheating boyfriends (me), a divorce (her) and a stabbing (me again) to name but a few. I've spent the last ten minutes telling her what happened with Darren this evening.

'Yeah, he is a prick,' I agree. 'We were going to break up sooner or later so it may as well have ended with me punching his head.' Charlotte laughs loudly before slipping out of the booth to order another round. We've already had a couple of martinis and I'm starting to feel that familiar buzz as the alcohol is absorbed into my bloodstream.

'DI Erika Piper!' booms a voice behind me and I spin around to see who has called my name.

'Ah! Tommy Calder!' I reply, sliding out of the booth to give him a hug.

I've always enjoyed working with Tom, though we've never spent any time together outside of work. 'What brings you to Foragin?'

'I live here now, moved a few months ago. I'm just here with a few friends for a couple of birthday drinks. Are you here by yourself?'

I shake my head. 'No, my friend is at the bar getting more cocktails. We're drowning sorrows.'

'Nothing major I hope?'

For the second time tonight, I give an abridged version of the events of my night. His expression flits between sympathy and something I can't quite put my finger on. He laughs heartily when I tell him about punching Darren just as Charlotte returns with a tray comprising four martinis and two shot glasses full of what I believe is Sambuca, judging by the sickly aniseed scent.

'Heavy night planned?' asks Tom, ogling the contents of the tray.

'It's shaping up that way. Thankfully it's my day off tomorrow,' I reply, already fearing tomorrow's hangover.

Tom bids us goodbye and re-joins his friends at the back of the bar.

'He's a bit dishy, isn't he?' exclaims Charlotte.

I don't reply. I'd never thought of Tom that way before. Maybe it's because I'm a free woman now, if only for the past hour or so, or maybe it's the alcohol making its merry way through my veins, but she is right. She passes me one of the shot glasses.

'Sláinte!' she shouts before we gulp it down.

WE STUMBLE OUT THE door and onto the cold street outside. The taxi driver looks less than thrilled as Charlotte fiddles with the car door handle. She falls into the back seat and mumbles her address.

'Let me know when you get home safe,' I say.

She holds her phone against the window as the taxi pulls away. As I turn in the direction of my house, Tom and his friends exit the bar in a haze of conversation and laughter. He notices me and pulls away from the group, telling them he'll see them another time.

'Do you fancy one more drink?' he asks. 'I'm not ready to go home.'

I know I shouldn't as I've already drank way too much. In spite of this knowledge, my feet seem to be in charge and are already leading me back inside.

We grab a couple of the comfortable seats near the back. He orders the drinks and staggers back to the table with them. We clink our glasses and I take a small sip. He fills me in on some of the cases I've missed whilst I've been off, and I tell him about my operation and the aftermath of the attack. He's good company.

When we finish our drinks, he stands up and slips his wallet into the back pocket of his jeans whilst I gather my bag from under the table and attempt to stand up, almost toppling over the chair in the process.

Tom grabs me round the waist to stop me falling and I feel my heart flutter. Our eyes meet and the moment seems to last a lifetime before he lowers his lips to meet mine; a glorious feeling that has nothing to do with the alcohol.

'Shall I walk you home?' he asks softly.

7

ANOTHER ONE BITES THE DUST, the ring tone I have reserved for Liam, erupts from my phone and opens the gates of hell to my hangover. I pull my arm as quickly as I can from under the covers and try to grab the phone from my bedside table. I feel around in the darkness before realising that there is no bedside table.

The ringing of the phone stops but the ringing in my ears continues. I tentatively open one eye and confirm my suspicions; I'm not in my bedroom. This room is bathed in blue, cast from the standby light of a huge, wall mounted flat screen TV.

There are clothes strewn over the floor and an electric guitar leans against an oversized amplifier in the corner of the messy room. I fall back onto my pillow and squeeze my eyes tight, trying to reconstruct the past 12 hours. The introductory bassline from the Queen classic blasts from my phone again.

'Can't you shut that thing up?' mumbles a sleepy voice from beside me.

'Shhhh,' I reply, moving the phone towards my ear. I greet the caller without looking at the screen.

'I know it's your day off and I hate to be the bearer of bad news, but the boss wants to see us both this morning,' Liam says, his voice raised against the background noise of what I assume is the station.

'Jesus Liam, you don't have to yell,' I croak, the words barely escaping from my throat, 'I'll be there as soon as I can.'

I throw the phone on the bed and gently rise to a sitting position. My head is heavy and my eyes feel dry. I also note that I am naked. This may complicate matters. I turn my head slowly and notice Tom squinting at me.

'We're going to be water cooler fodder,' he rasps, smiling.

'We can't tell anyone about this, I already feel at a disadvantage having just come back to work. The last thing I need is more drama.'

'Don't worry,' he replies, 'it's between you and me.'

I thank him and slip a leg out from underneath the covers. 'Turn around, I need to get dressed.'

'What?' he laughs. 'But I saw everything last night!'

'Turn around!' He holds his hands up and follows my instruction, rolling over on the bed and shoving his face into the pillow. I shuffle out of bed and scrabble about on the floor, trying to locate the clothes I hastily discarded the night before.

When I've recovered the lost garments, I stand up and pull them on at record speed. Looking up once I've fastened my bra, I notice the mirror on the far wall reflecting Tom's gaze, fully focussed on me.

'You creep!' I hiss, before leaving the room with a wide smile.

DCI BOB LOVATT'S OFFICE is bigger than mine. A framed Lowry painting depicting matchstick men congregating outside a factory hangs pride of place on the wall behind his mahogany desk. DCI Bob is sitting in a high-backed swivel chair across from Liam and me. He's coming up to retirement age; a heavy-set man with ruddy cheeks, thinning grey hair and a carefully shaped goatee. Dark brown eyes are currently blazing in our direction and he is scowling at us.

'Late night?' he asks, looking pointedly at my heavy eyes, though he presses on without waiting for an answer. 'We let the director go. The blood on his overalls was theatrical blood; he used those overalls when he was filming particularly bloody scenes, which I believe are a trademark of his.'

Neither Liam nor I say anything. Bob continues 'Surprisingly, he didn't seem too upset about being detained. He requested that you ring him, Erika. I can only imagine that he wants an apology.'

He hands me a Post-it note with a mobile number scrawled on it, before flicking his hand at us, our signal to leave his office.

I close the door behind me and shuffle across the room to my office. When inside, I throw myself into the chair and lean back, staring at the ceiling. *Fooled by fake blood, what a fucking idiot*, I think to myself. Perhaps Liam and I had been a tad hasty in bringing Reuben to the station.

I swallow my pride, pick up the telephone receiver and dial the number. It rings for a matter of seconds before he answers it.

'Reuben, this is DI Erika Piper. You wanted me to ring you?'

'Ah detective! The magic of cinema, eh? Amazing what a bit of red food colouring can do,' he laughs, before taking on a more sombre tone. 'I just wanted to say no hard feelings. I want Anna's killer caught as much as you, and if a few hours in the cells rules me out, then I'm happy. I was just wondering...'

Suddenly, there's a commotion on the other end of the line.

'Is that the police?' shouts an American voice down the line.

'Yes, this is Detective...'

'I don't give a fuck what your name is!' he interrupts. 'Do you know how much money you cost me by taking Reuben away from set for no reason? He hasn't done anything wrong and you have wasted a day of filming. Don't you fucking dare turn up on set again, d'ya hear me?'

With that, the line goes dead. I try to phone back but it goes straight to voicemail.

I retrieve my notebook from my desk drawer and find my 'to do' list. At the bottom of the list I add 'find out more about the American.'

Once added, I peruse the list and wonder what the next step in the investigation should be. My hangover is trying to convince me that a few hours in my own bed is the sensible course of action to take, and I am well within my rights to leave, though I feel DCI Bob wouldn't be pleased with that decision. I decide instead to verify Reuben's story about what happened when the three musketeers left the bar together.

I turn on my computer and open up the CCTV file from outside Limas. I fast forward the footage until Anna, Reuben and the man, who must be Ed, emerge from the bar. Ed is about the same height as Reuben, but much thinner, and is wearing a shirt coupled with a smart jacket and jeans. A man-bag hangs at his side and bumps rhythmically against his leg as he walks. He's clean shaven with short, spiked hair.

The two men have a short discussion before they bid each other goodbye. Ed stands by the bus stop, whilst Anna and Reuben exit the screen. His eyes remain in the direction of his companions, presumably making sure that Reuben is managing OK.

After a few minutes, probably when they are out his view, he perches on the seat of the bus stop. He takes his phone out of his pocket, tapping and scrolling on it for a while whilst absent-mindedly picking his nose with the other hand.

Eventually, a bus pulls up and partially obscures the view of the street outside the bar for just over three minutes. When it pulls away from the kerb, Ed is gone. In the background, people enter Limas in small groups under the scrutiny of a couple of heavy-set bouncers.

In the doorway of the shop next door, a homeless man, who has recently arrived, adjusts himself on the cardboard he is using as a bed. I watch for a few more minutes but nothing of note happens. I exit the file, content that Ed has indeed boarded the bus as Reuben had claimed. I pick up the phone on my desk and ask Liam to come to my room.

'Get your coat, we're going to a hotel,' I say as he walks into the room.

'And I didn't even have to buy you dinner!' he replies. I roll my eyes.

WE'RE IN THE SECURITY control room (a rather grandiose term for a small office at the back of the building) of the hotel Reuben claimed he took Anna to after they'd left the bar. The tired-looking receptionist at the front desk couldn't find a reservation from Friday night under Anna's nor Reuben's name, so had shown us to this room and put us in the very capable hands of Steve.

Steve is a broad-shouldered man with a thick head of dark hair and smiling eyes. He taps the mouse until the computer screen shows the front desk from Friday evening. He whizzes through footage of the receptionist, a middle-aged man, trying everything in his power not to nod off.

Once the clock in the bottom corner approaches the time Reuben claims they left the bar, he slows the video down with a click of the mouse. We watch as the receptionist tidies the desk and sorts things away into drawers. He leaves the desk for a few minutes and returns with a cup of tea. We watch for a little while longer, though nothing of note happens and the time frame for Reuben and Anna's arrival passes. Steve speeds through the footage just to confirm they don't turn up later than expected.

'Do you have exterior cameras?' I ask Steve.

'We do,' he nods, 'but only on the front door. Would you like me to get the footage from Friday night?' he asks, already making his way to the folder containing the footage without waiting for an answer. He closes the front desk footage and clicks through a few files before a grainier image appears on screen.

'The outside camera isn't to the same spec as the indoor ones,' he says, sounding slightly apologetic, as he starts the footage. As the hotel is at the far end of the main precinct, there is very little footfall. A few people stagger in the direction of the bars further down the street.

After a few minutes, my interest is piqued; Anna and Reuben enter the screen. She has her arm around his neck and he is carefully guiding her towards the doors of the hotel. When they get close, he slides her off and places her on the step outside the doors. He presses the button to be let in, but nothing happens. Perhaps this is the period of time when the receptionist is making his tea.

Anna must say something because he turns to look at her. They appear to have a short conversation, during which he adopts quite aggressive body language. He takes out his wallet and hands her some notes, which she considers for a second before throwing it at him. He says something to her and she shakes her head. He holds his hands up before turning and walking down the street.

Anna rises to her feet and attempts to follow him into the darkness, though after a few steps stumbles and falls to her knees. She remains on the ground, unmoving, in this position for a few minutes.

On the wall adjacent to the hotel, a shadow grows and another body enters the footage, that of a man. He limps towards Anna and hoists her up, positioning her arm over his shoulder before leading her down the street and quickly out of view.

8

I PAUSE THE CCTV footage from outside Limas and point to the homeless man in the doorway with my pen.

'Do you think that's him?' I ask Liam.

He glances between the computer screen and a printout of the man who picked Anna up. It's a still from when he first enters the camera's field of vision from outside the hotel's entrance.

It's dark and grainy which makes it difficult to pick out any distinguishing features, though he does appear to have a patchy beard. The man outside the bar has his hood up and is shrouded in the darkness of the doorway, making it difficult to make a worthwhile comparison.

'It's hard to tell,' he replies, his eyes switching from screen to printout and back again.

I press play on the video in the hope that the homeless man huddled in the doorway does something of note. He shifts about on the cardboard in an apparent attempt to get comfortable against the biting cold of the December night.

After a minute or so, he seems to find the position he's looking for, as he curls up in a ball, his legs tucked in tight against his chest.

As I'm about to move the mouse to close the file, I freeze. Another homeless man, Zed, well known to the police, enters the video. He is carrying a plastic bag in his hand, and a holdall is slung over his shoulder. He is marching purposely towards the doorway housing the unknown homeless man.

When Zed reaches him, he shouts something and when the man doesn't react, grabs him by the collar, hoisting him to his feet. Even though Zed is a head shorter, the taller man, judging by his body language, is scared. They have a brief discussion and he nods his head in agreement with whatever Zed has said to him, lifts his bag and walks, with a slight limp, out of the video frame.

'The limp,' I say, tapping my finger on his trailing leg, 'that's our man. The guy who picked Anna up off the floor outside the hotel had a limp. I think we need to talk to Zed to see what he can tell us.'

Liam rubs a hand over his stubbly jaw. 'Another trip to Altrincham? We've only just got back!' he moans.

'Stop your whining,' I scold. 'You can tell me how your wedding plans are coming along and I'll treat you to lunch in that café you like there.'

'Pinonos? Now we're talking,' he says, hoisting himself out of his seat and heading towards the station doors like an eager puppy.

We walk in the direction of the car park and as we round the corner of the building, a man, who was two seconds ago leaning lazily against the wall of the station, leaps into the middle of the pavement, blocking our way.

'Alright,' he says, tipping his head forward in a mock-friendly way. 'Is it true you have arrested Reuben Amaro in connection with Anna Symon's murder?'

As he finishes his question, he pulls a notepad out of his jacket pocket and retrieves a biro that was resting upon his ear. He reminds me of one of the hyenas from The Lion King.

'No,' replies Liam, attempting to push past him. The journalist walks backwards, in step with us.

'Why did he come out of the station earlier then? Is he your prime suspect?'

We remain silent as we march towards him. He is still walking backwards and, because of this, doesn't see the lamppost until he has collided with it – his back smashing into the unyielding metal pole.

Liam and I step around him as he writhes in pain on the ground, his notepad and pen strewn across the floor. We reach the car and get in, just as he straightens himself with a look of discomfort on his face.

'You know this is only the start of press involvement unless we solve this quickly?' Liam says as we pull out of the station's car park towards the motorway.

IT DOESN'T TAKE LONG to find Zed; he is in his usual spot, sitting on his blanket against a stretch of wall between Marks and Spencer and Santander.

'How many times do I have to tell you Zed? You can't be hanging about near the ATMs.' I say in way of a greeting.

'Oh!' he says in his thick Scottish accent, looking around wildly, apparently clocking the money dispensing machines for the first time. 'I didnae realise that's what they are.'

Zed is, what my mother would call, a scally-wag. Straggly, ginger hair hangs over his face which is mostly obscured by a thick, matted beard. He has lost many teeth, whether to poor oral hygiene, or otherwise, is debatable.

A tatty puffer jacket, ripped waterproof trousers and scuffed boots are what he has cobbled together in an attempt to keep himself warm. His trademark Manchester United beanie hat completes his look; a hat he has worn constantly for as long as I've known him and has bequeathed him the moniker Zed the Red.

'I havenae done anything, officers,' he says, holding his hands up.

'No-one said you have,' I reply. 'We're here for your help.' At this, his eyes widen and brighten. The illusion of power has been handed to him.

'Oh aye? What's in it for me?' he asks.

'A hot lunch?'

I can sense his excitement at the prospect of a hearty meal, though he plays it visibly cool. 'Throw in dessert and you've got me for as long as you need me.'

'Sounds fair,' I reply, offering my hand to help him to his feet. He accepts and rises from the floor, slinging the bag which contains all his earthly belonging over his shoulder.

We walk past a number of bustling shops with Christmassy window displays before turning into a narrow side street on the left and approaching Liam's favourite deli.

I hold the door open, which the two men thank me for, and choose a table with a view of the cobbled lane. Zed snatches up one of the laminated menus and silently peruses his options.

I glance up and notice the woman behind the counter observing our table with a certain degree of disgust and I feel a pang of sympathy for our lunch guest. Thankfully, he is oblivious.

After a few minutes, she approaches the table with a notepad and pen, enquiring if we are ready to place our orders. Liam has his answer out almost before she has finished asking the question. 'I'll have the chicken pasta primo, please.'

'Make that two,' I add.

'Ummm…I'll have broccoli cheddar soup te start, the Chicken Alfredo for main and…' he pauses whilst he consults the dessert menu, 'I'll need a ween of minutes to decide on the cake.'

We add our drinks to the order and she leaves the table.

'A three-course meal? You best have some useful information!' Liam laughs.

I retrieve a still from my bag of the CCTV footage from outside Limas, featuring the unknown homeless man and Zed and push it under his nose. 'What can you tell us about this?'

'I didnae dae anything te'im!' shouts Zed, already on the defensive.

'OK, so talk us through what happened' I say, quietly, in the hope Zed will follow suit.

'Well, I was just up at the offie getting a bottle to help pass the night, you know? When Limas is open at the weekends, my mate Charlie and me like to watch the girls go by in their wee skirts so I was on my way to his house.'

'House?' I ask.

'Doorway,' he confirms. 'It's the one beside the bar, best view, so I was scootin' down there to meet him and I get there and some fucker is laying down on his card. I ask him politely to vacate the premises and when he doesn't make a move, I grab him and tell him in no uncertain terms where to go and what'll happen if I see him again. With that, he turns and limps up the other end of town.'

'Did you know the man?'

'No,' he shakes his head emphatically and puffs out his chest, 'and I'm a well-connected man, d'ye know what I mean? Anyone on the street I tend te know, and anyone on the street tends te knows me. That's why I was surprised to find someone in Charlie's space.'

'Could you describe him?' I venture.

He looks up at the ceiling with a tilted head. 'Aye. He had a shite beard, like a wee boy who hasn't had te shave yet but wants to keep a bit of fluff to impress his mates. He had his hood up but it looked like he was bald. Hard te tell 'cos he was fair tall. To be honest, he didn't seem homeless. Look at the state of me,' he says, motioning to his clothes, 'this is what fucking homeless looks like. Naw, this man had a pretty smart coat on, and not a mark on his boots.'

'Wow! You really took note of what he was wearing,' I joke. 'Are you a secret fashionista?'

'I was gonna rob him,' comes his very honest reply.

'Well, well done for making the right choice.' I say with a wry smile. 'And why didn't you rob him?'

'All things considered, I felt bad for him. I thought if he has these swanky threads on, he was probably new to the streets and I didn't want to be an arsehole to him, you know?'

'And what happened after he left? Did you see him again?'

'Naw, he disappeared up the street and I settled down in Charlie's house. He appeared shortly after with some cigarettes and we got an eyeful for a few hours.'

With that, he begins to describe what some of the girls going into the club were wearing, and I zone out. So this guy from the video might not even be homeless. But why would he be preparing to spend the night on the street? Was he waiting for Anna to leave the bar? Is it purely a coincidence and this poor man is newly homeless?

I take out my notepad and make a note, in capitals, to find the identity of this man as a priority.

As I am putting the notebook back in the bag, I glance out the window and nearly fall off my chair in shock. Emerging from a small hardware store on the opposite side of the street is none other than Rory Knox, Anna's fiancé.

9

'WHAT HAPPENED?' ASKS LIAM, as I re-enter the café twenty minutes later. Zed is no longer at the table and Liam has his hands wrapped around a filter coffee. I slump into my seat and ask the barista for a cappuccino before regaling Liam with my tale.

'I followed Rory at a distance through the high street and into the shopping arcade. He walked straight through it, without as much as a sideways glance, back to his car. From what I could see, he didn't have any other bags with him so I assume he only visited the town centre for the hardware store. Once he got to the car park, he unlocked his vehicle, a black Porsche, and drove off. I noted down his car registration and I've already sent it off to see what ANPR can tell us. I'm going to phone him and find out what he's up to.'

I take out my phone and find Rory's number. Liam nods and takes a sip from his coffee cup as the phone starts to ring.

'Hello,' Rory's familiar voice answers.

'Hi Rory, this is DI Erika Piper, how are you?'

'So-so.' He sounds angry, the fuzzy background noise and the echoic voices tells me I must be on loudspeaker.

'I was just ringing to find out if a Family Liaison Officer had been in touch yet.' Liam smiles at my sneakiness.

'Not yet,' he replies, curtly.

'OK, well I'll make a note to chase that up for you. Have I caught you at a bad time?'

'My fiancée was murdered a few days ago,' he says, 'did you think you were going to catch me at a good time? Have you found who killed her yet?'

'Not yet,' I confess. 'Are you still in Manchester?' I ask, and when there is no reply, I check the phone's screen to find that the call has been disconnected.

Without a word to Liam, I use the internet to search for the company Rory works for in London. I find it and call, pressing the phone to my ear. A receptionist with a high-pitched, grating voice greets me with the well-known company's name, followed by her own. I ask to speak to Rory but I'm told he is on compassionate leave and probably won't be in the office for at least another two weeks, though if I would like to speak to a colleague, she'd be more than happy to put me through. I tell her that my query can wait, thank her and hang up.

I recount the phone conversations to Liam and we discuss the possible reasons as to why Rory is still hanging about the north of England. Perhaps he wants to be here when we crack the case and he's being optimistic about the timescale. Perhaps the reason for his prolonged stay is altogether more menacing.

'You think we should bring him in?'

'Not yet,' I reply, 'he's obviously lingering for a reason. Let's see what the ANPR tells us about where he is travelling to. That way, we will have more information to question him with. Let's get back to the office; I think we are due a briefing.'

DCI BOB STANDS AT the front of the briefing room, his sleeves are rolled up and his shirt is partially untucked at the front. He seems stressed, his face flushed and his words pouring out a little quicker than usual. He is underlining the importance of making headway in the case as the press are starting to poke their noses in and he can't give them an adequate enough answer to satisfy them. Once he feels he has emphasised his point, he hands the floor over to me.

I pull the evidence board into the centre of the room. It contains photos of Rory, Ed, Reuben, the unknown homeless man and the shoe print ingrained on Anna's face. I point to Rory and tell the assembled team about the latest encounter with the grieving fiancé and the plan to see what information we can gather through ANPR before bringing him in for questioning. In the corner of my eye, I can see the DCI nodding his head at this course of action.

Next, I motion to the grainy image of the homeless man and recount to the team what we know so far from the CCTV footage and from what Zed had to say. I make it priority number one to find him and confirm his identity. DCI Bob interjects and says he can try to get a few more officers into Altrincham town centre to try and locate him. With nothing left to report on him, I move onto the shoe print.

'Angela has managed to get something from this,' I say, pointing at the photo of Anna's cheek. 'Even though it is a partial print, Angela is certain it's a size twelve boot. The tread is consistent with those found on Caterpillar Shiftstick boots.

We think the killer bought them new very recently as the print shows no signs of wear and tear. It could have been the first time he's ever worn them. This theory is in keeping with what Zed said about the homeless man wearing boots that didn't have a scuff on them.'

I turn to Angela.

'Any luck getting through to Ed?' I ask.

She stands up and faces the team.

'I haven't been able to get through to him personally, though I do have a mobile number for him. It keeps going to voicemail. His agent has confirmed that he has travelled to the Scottish Highlands for a writing retreat. It started the day after Anna was murdered and finishes today, so we may have a chance of getting in touch with him either later today or tomorrow. He has that joint event with the director,' she points at the picture of Reuben, 'in The Book Club in Manchester the day after tomorrow.'

'Might it be an idea to have some police presence at the event?' asks the DCI to the room.

'Good idea, Chief,' I say, 'I'm happy to go. Reuben seems to think I'm alright, despite falsely accusing him of murder.' The room fills with laughter. I think we can rule him out as a suspect now. His alibi has been confirmed.'

'I'm happy to go too,' chimes Tom. 'I'm a fan of *The Threat* books so it'll be interesting for me to see what the author is up to next.'

'It's a date!' says the Chief, a hint of a smile in the upturned corners of his mouth. Is that a knowing smile or am I being paranoid?

'Right everyone, next steps; monitor Rory's movements once the ANPR hits come in and find out who this homeless, or fake homeless, or whatever, man is.'

He turns as if to return to his office, before calling, 'Erika, my room please.'

'I KNOW YOU'RE NOT going to like this' is never a good opening gambit, but it's what the Chief has opted for.

'I've arranged for you to have counselling,' he says gently. 'What you went through last year was horrific, and I think you should discuss what you are feeling with a professional.'

I know his intentions are well meaning, though I still let out a loud sigh.

'I suppose I don't have a choice?' I ask, sounding slightly like a stroppy teenager.

'You don't, I'm afraid. I have a duty of care to my staff and I think this will be very beneficial for you. Your first session is this evening,' he adds, with the hint of an apologetic smile.

WHEN I IMAGINE COUNSELLING, I revert to the stereotypes; an old, bearded man with glasses perched on the end of his nose nodding at everything I say with an expressionless face, a leather chaise-longue and extended stretches of silence which I am expected to break.

My pigeonholing daydream is broken by a woman coming out of an office separated from the waiting room by a heavy wooden door with a patterned, stained glass window. She is roughly the same age as me – early thirties – wearing a knee length floral dress and a pair of shiny court shoes.

'Would you like to come through?' she asks.

I nod and enter the office. The light blue walls are mostly bare, with one large photograph of a beautiful stretch of empty beach meeting calm, blue sea hanging on the far wall beside a large window. Her desk is uncluttered, a notepad and a small digital clock the only objects on it.

She motions to a vacant, white and green striped chair with plump cushions, into which I duly sink. She sits in an identical chair opposite me, though it is slightly tilted away from mine so as not to enforce unwanted eye contact.

'My name is Doctor Vaughn, though I prefer to be called Amy. I am here to help you in any way I can. Why don't you start by telling me why you're here and what you would like to get out of these sessions,' she says.

'I'm here because my boss made me come,' I say, haughtily, despite liking Amy from the outset.

'And why did your boss make you?' she replies in the same measured tone as her introduction.

I sigh. I've not talked about what happened in the warehouse with anyone I know. It has remained a secret which I've kept locked away for fear of not coping. For fear of people thinking that I'm weak.

Over the course of the next hour, the floodgates open and I expose myself to Amy in an unparalleled way. I disclose all my anxieties, I touch on what happened after the man emerged from the shadows in the warehouse and I confide in her my fears for the future; my anguish about the almost impossible chance of becoming a mother.

Once I finish, I feel lighter, like a massive weight has been lifted from my shoulders. I thank Amy for her time and we shake hands, arranging an appointment for the forthcoming week.

Entering the brisk evening air, I feel a rare sense of freedom I've not experienced since before the attack. Even though it's only the start of the process, I can sense a retreat of the dark thoughts that have clouded my mind for the past ten months.

I take my phone from my pocket and turn it on, plugging my headphones in and selecting a Bon Iver album to keep me company on my walk home. I shove it back in my pocket and begin the short walk. The time passes quickly, my thoughts on the case and the homeless man and before I know it, I'm on my driveway.

I plunge the key into the lock and it turns with a clunk. I walk in and call out Darren's name, to tell him I'm home, before realising he's not here and is probably gone for good. A mixture of emotions mingle in my stomach. Perhaps it was a mistake to break up with him, maybe he was right; maybe I hadn't tried hard enough in the aftermath of the attack. Then I rebuke myself. He'd suggested that having the chance of becoming a mother literally stabbed away from me was nothing more than unfortunate. I decide that I have made the correct decision after all, and that he can go and fuck himself.

Feeling emotionally drained after my first counselling session, I drag myself up the stairs and fall into bed, fully clothed. I plug the charger into my phone and place it on the bedside table having set my alarm for the morning. I drift off within seconds.

10

THE JOLLY ALARM TONE rings out through the darkness, wandering into my dream like an unwelcome visitor, cutting it short. I grope in the general direction of the noise, unwilling to open my eyes, and hit the snooze button, allowing myself the luxury of an extra ten minutes under the duvet. Pulling the covers over my head, I contemplate the day ahead of me, one I've selfishly been dreading for a few months; my sister's baby shower.

I feel guilty for feeling this way; for a long time, I wasn't even sure I wanted to have children. In my early twenties, I was so focussed on my career, striving to get as far as possible as quickly as I could. The thought of having children hadn't even been considered. Surely they'd just hold me back, prevent me from doing the thing I'd trained for years to do.

As I'd entered my late twenties, the pitter patter of tiny feet started to become something of a consideration. My career had progressed in accordance to my expectations and I'd been with a caring boyfriend for a number of years. The time felt right.

And then, a year ago, almost all hope of ever being a mother had been snatched away from me. Now, it's all I want. I long to hold a baby, my baby, as it drifts off to sleep in my arms. I yearn for time spent chasing the little one as it toddles around a garden in full bloom and my heart breaks each and every time I realise that this will probably never, ever happen.

When the alarm sounds again, I force myself out of bed, recoiling as my bare feet make contact with the frigid wooden floorboards. I grab a fresh towel from the airing cupboard and head to the bathroom, stepping into the shower and enjoying the hot water cascading over my body. I stay in the shower for longer than necessary and when I'm done, I dry myself quickly and pull on the dress I save for special occasions.

There's an ulterior motive for wearing the slightly low-cut frock; the event at The Book Club is tonight and I want to make an effort for Tom.

Once I've slipped into it, I lie back down on the bed with my hair in a towel and consider what is happening between Tom and me. I don't even know if I *want* anything to develop with him. It's so soon after Darren and I had decided to call it a day, though it feels like we have been separated for a lot longer. I'm not sure Tom wants anything to happen either. Conceivably, a drunken fumble was all that he wanted. Still, best to look the part.

I decide to let my hair dry naturally so I walk down the stairs and gobble down a quick brunch before leaving the house and heading towards the train station.

I TAKE A STEADYING breath and knock on Sarah's door. My sister lives in a red brick end-of-terrace on a quiet cul-de-sac in Didsbury, a desirable suburb in South Manchester. A silhouette appears in the frosted glass, growing as the figure reaches the door. Sarah's husband, Will, answers and greets me with a hug. He is holding a jacket in one hand and car keys jangle in the other.

'Good luck,' he says with a devilish grin.

'Have you managed to worm your way out of staying?'

'Indeed I have, I'm going golfing,' he replies, wiping his brow in mock relief. 'It's a ridiculous Americanism that I want no part of. Though I am grateful for the presents!' he adds hastily, eyeing the present in my hand.

With that, he walks towards his BMW, starts the ignition and reverses out of the driveway with a beep of his horn. I walk in and announce my arrival. Sarah, smiling, appears at the far end of the hallway, motioning to join her in the kitchen.

'Oh, you look fancy,' she trills, looking me up and down and caressing the silky material of my dress. 'A bit sexy for a baby shower isn't it?'

Sarah and I could be twins, but for the two-year age gap. We both have dark brown hair, though I have let mine grow beyond my shoulders and she is currently sporting a bob. We share green eyes, a slight build and sadly, the Piper family overbite.

She opens the door of the American style fridge and retrieves a bottle of Moët & Chandon, the one her office stupidly bought her for going on maternity leave. The cork leaves the bottle with a loud pop and some of the sparkling liquid spills onto the floor. She hands me an empty glass and starts to pour, ignoring my protestations about having to work later.

'Thanks for being here, Erika,' she says, clinking her glass of orange juice onto mine. 'I know this can't be easy for you, but it means the world to me that you are here. Especially since mum...you know...' she trails off and dabs at the corner of her eye with a paper napkin.

'Last year was hard for everyone. I wouldn't be anywhere else today.' I give her shoulder a squeeze before grabbing a cloth from the sink and mopping up the spilled champagne.

'It's been a while since we caught up,' she says as I drape the cloth over the tap, 'how is it being back at work?'

'It's good. It feels good to have a routine again. I'm guessing you heard about Anna Symons?'

'Heard about it? I've bought every gossip magazine I can get my hands on. I've even watched the news religiously, which you know I hate! Everyone reckons it's the fiancé. Do you think he did it?'

'You know I can't possibly discuss the case, even with you,' I say, digging her gently in the ribs with my elbow, fully aware of the baby bump.

'Have you met him?' she asks, pushing my arm away.

'Yes.'

'Is he as sexy in real life as he is in photos?'

Until now, I hadn't thought about it. 'I suppose he is, yes. He came in to the station all suited and booted, looked like a movie star himself.'

'I bet it *is* him. Documentaries always say it's the victim's partner. Maybe he's a Ted Bundy type, charming and handsome but fucking dangerous!'

'I bet no other baby shower in the country has ever started with a Ted Bundy reference. I came early to help you set up, not debate a case I'm not allowed to talk about.' I scold. 'Now,' I say, taking on a kinder tone, 'what do you need me to do?'

She looks dismayed.

For the next half an hour we work hard to make the house baby shower ready. When we are done, pastel coloured bunting hangs from doorways and an array of food is positioned invitingly on the table in the front room. Once our glasses are topped up, we flop down on the sofa and await the arrival of the other guests.

'How does Darren feel about you being back at work?' Sarah asks, taking a sip from her glass.

'We've broken up,' I reply.

'Oh no,' she says, though she doesn't look too disappointed. 'Are you OK?'

'Yeah, I'm fine. It's been a long time coming.'

'It has, he has been a dick for a long time now.'

I snort with laughter. She never really saw eye to eye with Darren so I imagine she is pleased with the news. She continues unabated:

'So. Young, free and single for the first time in years! Men of Manchester, beware!'

She looks sideways at me and noticing my expression, sighs.

'Please don't tell me you've met someone new already?'

I proceed to fill her in about what happened after Darren and I broke up. When I finish, she shakes her head.

'Well, you did the right thing. You can't let a good set of lingerie go to waste. How was the se…'

A loud set of knocks on the door make us both jump.

'Saved by the bell,' Sarah says, pushing herself up in stages from the sofa, 'but we shall return to the juicy details later.'

She points a finger at me as she leaves the room.

The baby shower passes quickly in a hail of champagne and gifts. The highlight was watching Sarah try and pretend that she liked a few of the presents I know she had already earmarked for taking back, having pocketed the gift receipt.

At half past six, another knock on the door interrupts Sarah pouring yet another round of drinks for her, by now, very merry guests. She walks down the hallway and opens the door, before shouting my name. I collect my belongings and make my way towards the door, ignoring Sarah's furtive glances.

Standing at the open door is Tom, who is here to pick me up and drive us to The Book Club in the city centre. He is wearing a blue shirt tucked into a pair of maroon chinos. I give Sarah a hug and bid her farewell.

'So that's why you're wearing that dress,' she whispers to me as I step out the door, though I pretend I haven't heard her.

'Have a good night, you two! Behave yourselves!' she shouts after us as we walk down the path towards the gate. I spin around and hold my hand up, middle finger protruding.

We walk to his car which is parked just around the corner and I slide into the passenger seat, slamming the door shut as Tom turns his key in the ignition.

Whilst he is setting the sat nav, I pull my phone out of my bag, having realised I haven't checked it all afternoon. I'm surprised to see a message from Sarah. Maybe I've forgotten something. I open the message and feel my face flush at its content.

It doesn't take a detective to understand what a GIF of Churchill the Dog chanting 'Oh Yes' over and over again is in reference to. I sneak a glance at Tom – who has pretended not to notice the dog's incantation, though he does have a wide smile on his face – before making a mental note to kill my sister.

11

THE BOOK CLUB IS a small, independent book shop located on a side street in the Northern Quarter area of Manchester. If you weren't actively seeking it out, it's possible you'd never set eyes on it. The lime green sign above our heads shows the shop's name in bold lettering and the window display on one side of the door is dedicated to debut authors and books from indie publishers.

On the other side of the door, the books all share a Mancunian theme; either books about the rich history of the city or literature showcasing home-grown talents.

The small shop has a homely feel. Wooden bookshelves line each of the four walls, proudly housing books of every genre from floor to ceiling. Colourful pieces of card are sporadically placed, giving recommendations from the staff as to what they think you should read next.

A small desk with a cash register has been placed in the centre of the room, taking up as little space as possible to allow maximum exposure of the merchandise.

We enter the shop and a friendly member of staff greets us just inside the door with a glass of prosecco, which I decline, having already had a few earlier in the day.

She informs us that the event will be starting soon, and points us in the direction of the staircase which is through a doorway I hadn't previously noticed at the back of the shop.

We thank her and make our way towards the stairs, weaving through a few stragglers who are scanning the shelves, lost in the land of books. At the bottom of the stairs, another employee is checking the tickets for the sold-out event.

A harried man with thick, bushy hair in front of us is riffling through his trouser pockets, double checking and still coming up empty. The employee looks over the man's shoulder at us and gives us a knowing, exasperated look.

Finally, the man locates his ticket in the breast pocket of his raincoat. He hands the slightly soggy ticket to the employee who motions for him to ascend the stairs. Tom already has the tickets in his hand and flashes them, before standing aside to let me climb the stairs before him.

There is already a buzz of excitement in the upstairs function room. Framed covers of famous novels adorn the wood-panelled walls and a single light on the ceiling bathes the room in a dim glow. A narrow aisle bisects the room and a table at the back has been set up to showcase a variety of merchandise including the three books in *The Threat* series.

Approximately sixty foldable plastic chairs have been laid out in rows and most have been already been claimed. Tom and I scan for any remaining seats and, locating two together at the end of the back row, squeeze by eager attendees to reach them. I set my bag and coat on the floor and kick them underneath my seat, before settling into the uncomfortable chair.

'Have you read any of Ed's books?' asks Tom. 'They're pretty good.'

I shake my head. 'I hadn't even heard of him until we started investigating this case.'

Looking around, I notice it's a strange mixture of people who have gathered for the event. Two girls in Goth get up sit beside an old man who is tapping rhythmically on his walking stick. In front of them sit an entire row of men in suits, and at the end of the front row is a man I recognise - Jay, the rude American from the film set at Conwy. He is wearing a tight shirt tucked untidily into black suit trousers. He is so wide that his bulk is taking up almost two seats and spilling out into the aisle. I decide to corner him at the end of the night and reprimand him for how he spoke to me on the phone a few days ago.

A few minutes later, a petite woman with short blond hair and round, oversized glasses walks down the aisle towards the three upholstered seats and a low table at the end of the room, situated on a raised platform serving as a stage.

On the table sits a laptop and a rectangular metal frame, from which two microphones dangle. There are also three glasses of water at the other end of the table, presumably positioned as far away from the electrical equipment as possible in case of spillage.

She lifts a microphone from the floor of the stage and taps the end of it with a manicured nail. The speakers, one either side of the stage, broadcast the rhythm a little too loudly around the small room. Conversations stop as screechy feedback interrupts them.

'Do I need to use this?' she asks the room, holding the microphone aloft. The crowd answer with a unanimous no, so she flicks the power switch and sets the microphone down again.

'Right,' she says, unamplified, smiling at the crowd. 'My name is Julia and I am going to be your host for the evening. Thank you so much for coming to this wonderful event. What a night we have in store!'

A few people around the room clap.

Julia continues, 'We are very lucky to be joined tonight by two men who have made their mark on the world of storytelling over the past few years. It's such a rare and wonderful opportunity to listen to these artists in such an intimate space. Shall we get them out?'

To this, the room erupts into a chorus of yeses and the two men we are here to see emerge from a side door near the front of the room.

They stride to their seats, taking their places, one on either side of Julia, who has placed herself in the middle chair. Reuben is wearing a very similar outfit to when we first met in Conwy, though he has lost the hat and has made an attempt to tame his shaggy hair. Ed is wearing a white shirt and black skinny jeans, both of which emphasize how thin he is.

'What an introduction!' says Reuben.

'Yeah, I feel you've oversold us Julia,' Ed declares, clean shaven and boyish, wagging a finger at the host. 'I hope we aren't a let-down!'

The room breaks into laughter.

'So,' continues Ed, 'tonight is the first of four events around the country and we thought we'd start with a hometown show. As you can see, we have some equipment on the stage,' he motions to the computer. 'Our plan is to record this and put this out as a podcast, so that people who can't make the event can still hear our news. So, for the sake of the podcast, we'd love it if you could give it the big one – clapping, cheering, that kind of thing.'

'Make it sound like you're having fun, even if you're not,' Reuben chimes in, eliciting more laughter from the crowd.

Ed then asks for silence in the room as he sets about starting the recording on the computer. He performs a microphone check and gives a thumbs up to Reuben, before launching into the introduction. When he raises his hands, the crowd go wild at his invitation and he flashes a wide smile of appreciation.

Ed looks over at Reuben to continue the introduction but the director isn't paying attention, instead, he's gawping at the top of the stairs at the back of the room.

'Sorry I'm late,' says the detached voice of a man I cannot see.

'Don't be silly, love,' replies Julia, 'we've only just started. There is a seat right here with your name on it,' she says to the man with a smile, pointing to a seat in the middle of the front row.

His footsteps on the polished wooden floor echo around the small room as he makes his way up the aisle.

He reaches his seat as Julia begins speaking again, and spends a minute removing his coat and scarf, and placing them carefully in front of his seat. All the while, Reuben hasn't looked away from the man once, and for good reason. The man taking his seat in the front row, directly in front of the director, is none other than Rory Knox.

Julia continues to address the audience and informs them of the running order of the evening, oblivious to the mounting tension in the room. Reuben has now broken eye contact with Rory and is looking at his shoes. Jay is staring at Rory who still has his eyes firmly fixed on the director.

I'm not sure if Ed has noticed what is happening, or whether he is trying to carry on with the show for Reuben's sake, but he has taken over from Julia and is currently regaling the crowd with an anecdote about his writing process.

There are small pockets of laughter, but I'm not sure why because I can't focus on his words. All of my attention is focussed on the unfolding situation. When he finishes, Julia turns to Reuben but before she can speak, she is interrupted.

'I've got a question,' states Rory.

Julia looks put out. 'There's a Q and A at the end, love, can it wait until then?'

'It won't take long,' he replies, turning from her to the director. 'Reuben, why did you kill my fiancée, Anna Symons?'

There is a collective gasp in the room. People in the audience glance at each other, but no one utters a word for fear of missing a second of the drama.

Reuben though, looks calm, like he expected this question from the moment Rory walked in.

'I didn't kill her,' he says, evenly. 'It's true that I was with her on the night she died. Not by my design though. She showed up at the same bar that Ed and I were in. Purely coincidental. She got very drunk and, for her own safety, I took her to a hotel and paid for her to stay the night. I'm very sorry for your loss, Rory, I truly am, but I am not the guilty party. Now, if you are here to derail the evening, I'm going to have to ask you to leave.'

Rory rises from his seat and takes a step towards Reuben, shaking his head. 'Ask me to leave?' he spits, 'I bought my ticket, I've got as much right to be here as everyone else. You admitted to fucking her all those years ago, now be a man and admit to killing her.'

As he takes another step towards Reuben, Jay stands up and manoeuvres himself between the two men. The audience still haven't made a single sound, though every unblinking eye is fixed on the action.

'I think it's time to head off now, pal,' says Jay in his American drawl, patting Rory on the chest.

Rory pulls away from him, seemingly disgusted.

'Don't you fucking touch me!' he bellows, pushing his forehead into Jay's. 'You're as much to blame for her death as him!'

Tom shuffles in his seat in anticipation of having to intervene, but two of the suited men who were sitting in the row behind Jay have jumped to their feet and are attempting to separate Rory and Jay before things take an even more violent turn.

They lead a flailing Rory down the aisle and out of view, though his loud protestations can still be heard for a few more minutes before gradually fading. Jay stares in the direction of the stairs and looks like he is about to follow, but instead sinks into his seat.

'Shall we take five?' Julia asks meekly.

12

FOLLOWING A HASTILY ARRANGED coffee break, Reuben, Ed and Julia have been back on stage for about half an hour and have been trying to continue with the show, despite the slightly distracted atmosphere in the room.

Julia is trying to keep the energy up but I can tell she has been rattled by the events of the evening so far. Reuben seems downcast and keeps his involvement to a minimum, relying on Ed to carry the show, which he is attempting to do gallantly.

'And now,' he says, taking on a more sombre tone. 'We really did put a lot of thought into whether or not to do these events in light of what happened to poor Anna. We didn't want to seem insensitive, but in the end, we decided that we didn't want to let you down. Before we continue with the evening, we would like to ask you to observe a minute's silence in her memory.'

A mournful silence is impeccably observed by everyone in the room, aside from someone near the front who suffers an unfortunately timed coughing fit.

I close my eyes and think of her body, the exposed skin frozen to the ice and the lifeless eyes, the untold violence she was subjected to in her final minutes. Ed speaks to signify the end of the minute and when I look at him, I can see that his eyes have filled with tears.

'Death is such a cruel mistress,' he says, and I can't tell if he is being genuine or whether he is trying to sound dramatic for the sake of the podcast.

'Now,' he says with renewed vigour. 'The whole purpose of this joint tour is that we each have an announcement to make.' He looks over at Reuben. 'Shall I go first?'

Reuben gives a slight nod of his head and Ed turns back to look at the crowd, playing the ringmaster.

'It's not the X-Factor, get on with it!' heckles someone near the front, drawing riotous laughter. Ed breaks into a huge smile.

'You can tell it's a Friday night in Manchester! OK, well after the final book in *The Threat* trilogy came out, I announced my retirement from writing. Well, I'm sorry to say I was a bit premature in announcing that. I was burnt out and a bit jaded with the whole process. But over the past two years, ideas began to percolate and I started tentatively writing a little bit each day and I fell in love with the process again, so I am delighted to announce that I have a new book on the way! I'm not going to give too much away, but I can confirm that it is a novella that is set between the third and fourth *Threat* books.'

The audience launch into a loud round of applause.

'It should be out around mid-July and the fourth full length *Threat* book is scheduled for release roughly around this time next year,' Ed continues once the clapping has abated, 'I literally emailed the final copy of the novella to the publishers this morning so I'm feeling a huge sense of relief. And now, Reuben!'

'Thanks Ed,' Reuben starts, much less enthusiastically. 'Well, as you may or may not know, the second film in *The Threat* series, *Hell Hammer*, is out next week.'

An excited cheer erupts.

'We're having a premiere in the Trafford Centre Odeon next Wednesday and you could win two tickets. We'll tell you how at the end of the evening. My announcement, and it feels a little ill timed, is that I have been tasked with directing the final *Threat* film.'

Another cheer erupts, however a young man, probably around twenty years old, sitting a few seats to my left is shaking his head. His left hand shoots up in the air and Reuben points at him.

'Why?' the man asks.

'Why what?' Reuben replies.

'Why have you got the job? *The Threat* was such a good book but the film adaptation was dreadful. You left out loads of important bits and royally fucked up the murder scenes. How have you managed to stay in a job?'

Reuben looks furious.

'What's your name?'

'Ben,' the man answers, his self-assuredness on parade as he puffs out his chest.

I can't help but think that he must be very brave or very stupid to be picking a fight, publicly, with someone who is clearly not in a good mood.

'Well, Ben, I'm sorry that you didn't enjoy the film and I agree, the book is amazing, in fact, the whole series is, and I feel very lucky that I've had the opportunity to bring them to

'Now, talk me thorough why you had such a go at Reuben and Jay?' I say when we are both perched on the cold metal.

'Well, I love *The Threat* books so much that when I heard they were going to turn them into a film, I got so excited. I'd read those books as a young teenager so they left an imprint, you know? But when *Blood Ice*, shit name by the way, came out, it was so bad. I was so disappointed. He – Reuben,' he elaborates, noticing my quizzical expression, 'got it so wrong. He missed out key points from the book and fucked up the things he left in. Anna's death scene was a pivotal moment in the book, but played such a minor scene in the film. The fact he got her naked for it too ruined the whole thing.'

'He said that wasn't his decision.'

'He's the fucking director, of course it's his decision,' he snorts.

'If you had been the director, would you have done her death scene differently?'

His eyes light up and when he speaks it's with wild enthusiasm. 'I would have been true to the book. I've read the book, and that chapter in particular so many times I know the scene inside out.'

This extremism alarms me. *Why is he so hung up on this particular section of the book?*

'Do you know how Anna died? In real life, I mean.'

'Yeah,' he nods, 'I heard on the radio that the killer created the scene from the film. Bet he did a better job than Reuben.' My eyes widen. 'Sorry,' he says, 'I know that's a weird thing to say but as a film student, I've fantasised about re-[...]g that scene, properly, to do it justice.'

life. I suggest that if you are not a fan of the films, don't bother going to see them.'

Ben does not look appeased.

'Why did you insist on Anna being naked in the film? She wasn't naked in the book and it seemed like a gratuitous choice to me.'

'Are you a fucking film critic?' asks Reuben, getting to his feet.

'No, I'm studying film making at university, but I don't need a degree to have an opinion.'

'True,' Reuben fires back, 'and you are perfectly entitled to one. The studio insisted on that particular aspect of the scene. I, if you must know, wanted to remain true to the book. Jason here,' he points to the huge American in the front row, 'works for the studio. He's the man with the money and, in essence, he has the final say. And in this business, money talks.'

'So you're saying he's to blame?'

Jay swivels in his chair and eyeballs Ben, who seems to shrink a little.

'Look pal,' his American accent booming in the small room. 'No one's to blame. I'm very proud of that movie and it made a lot of money at the box office.'

'Money doesn't equal success,' retorts Ben.

Knowing Jay's temperament, I wonder if Ben is putting himself in an unenviable position without realising. On cue, Jay rises to his feet and takes a step towards Ben.

'Get the fuck outta here you little punk!' he shouts, 'before I make you!'

Ben looks visibly shaken, which is perfectly natural considering Jay's mass. He grabs his bag from under his seat and moves towards the door. He opens his mouth and it looks like he is going to leave with a parting shot but seemingly thinks better of it and slinks down the staircase without another word.

'OK,' says Ed, 'I think we best leave it there for tonight.'

A few disappointed groans ring out.

'Thank you very much for coming. There is a leaflet downstairs with information about how to win tickets to the premiere of *Hell Hammer*.'

It's almost imperceptible but when he says the name of the film, I could swear he grimaces.

'I realise we haven't done the Q and A, so if anyone has anything to ask, I'll be downstairs in a few minutes and will be happy to answer any questions.'

He taps a few buttons on the computer, gets up from his seat, waves at the applauding crowd and leaves through the side door. Reuben follows him without as much as one last look at the audience.

TOM AND I MILL around the downstairs area waiting for Ed to finish talking to his legion of fans. He spends a generous amount of time answering questions, signing books and posing for selfies. Out of the corner of my eye, I spot Ben through the window, loitering outside the shop with a cigarette in his hand.

'Tom, I'm just going to grab Ben and find out if he knows anything about Anna. I know it's a long shot,' I say, gauging his reaction, 'but, at the minute, we've not got a suspect which means everyone is a suspect. Anything is worth a go.'

He nods his head.

'Fair point. You talk to Ben and I'll wait for Ed to finish with his fan club and get him to come down to the station to finally answer a few questions.'

I button up my coat and reluctantly leave the warmth of the bookshop, emerging onto the freezing street. Above my head, multi-coloured Christmas lights criss-cross between buildings, bathing the street in a vivid glow and lending the city centre a festive feel.

It appears that the shops on this particular street are embroiled in a competition of who can display the most elaborately decorated Christmas tree. Ben's back is to me and when I call his name, he jumps and spins around, surprised.

'Ben, my name is Detective Inspector Erika Piper. Would you mind answering a few questions?'

The unwavering confidence he displayed when accosting Reuben for his directorial abilities upstairs a short while has vanished at the sight of a police badge.

Ben is tall at about six feet, though his features almost-childlike. He has a beanie hat pulled tight over though some long curls haven't managed to be con peek out from underneath. He is sporting some facial hair; a poor attempt at a moustache and sideburns.

'Uh, yeah. Am I under arrest?' he asks, nerv

I almost smile at his greenness.

'No. I'd just like to find out a little mo were saying upstairs. Shall we sit?'

I motion to a nearby bench and wait steps before following him.

As I'm about to inform Ben that, based on this tête-à-tête, we need a more formal conversation at the station, a commotion from the bookshop interrupts us. Reuben is storming towards us with Ed grabbing at his arms and shoulder to try and prevent his arrival, to no avail.

Tom is a few steps behind, pushing past the crowd that has spilled out onto the street. Reuben pushes Ed to the side and, with a dull thud, lands a punch on the side of Ben's face which sends him sprawling off the bench and onto the cold ground. He grasps the side of his face and scrambles backwards, frantically trying to get to his feet as Reuben advances, fist held aloft.

As he is about to land another blow, Tom tackles him around the waist and attempts to pin him to the floor. I run to Tom's aid and help restrain Reuben as handcuffs are attached around his wrists and he is placed under arrest.

Pushing back the hair that has fallen over my eyes, I glance around at the bench and, to my annoyance, Ben is nowhere to be seen.

13

I'M STRUGGLING TO KEEP my eyes open this morning, having only managed to cram in a few hours' sleep before returning to my desk. Dealing with the Reuben situation crept into the early hours of the morning, and the clock on the bottom corner of my computer monitor currently displays 8:03 a.m.

I reach for my second coffee of the day, praying the caffeine kicks in sooner rather than later. Liam, fresh faced and sprightly, knocks on the door to my office and enters without waiting for an answer, throwing himself into one of the comfortable chairs, the water in his glass sloshing over the sides and spilling onto his trousers in the process.

'I hear Reuben has been a naughty boy again,' he says by way of a good morning greeting, whilst rubbing the wet patch with the back of his tie.

'He was, but in a way, I'm on his side,' I reply, receiving a perplexed look in return.

I spend the next few minutes filling my partner in on the events of the previous evening; how Rory and Ben proceeded to put a dampener on Reuben and Ed's special evening. How

Reuben, having been processed, paid his own bail and left the station looking ashamed. When I finish, Liam looks thoughtful.

'I see what you mean. This Ben fella sounds like he deserved that punch.' He takes a sip of water. 'So, all the big players were present; Reuben, Jay, Ed and Rory. And now this lad, Ben. Did you manage to talk to the illusive Ed?'

I shake my head.

'Tom was waiting for him while I had a word with Ben. We were going to bring Ed into the station for a chat, just to get his version of events from the night Anna died. But with everything that happened with Reuben and Ben, he was long gone by the time we got everything tied up. I have spoken to him this morning though and he has invited us to his house this afternoon.'

'Shouldn't we get him in here? Put a bit of pressure on?'

I consider this.

'To be honest, I don't think he's involved. And if I'm wrong, people are always more relaxed in their own home, more likely to give something away.' Liam nods his agreement.

'So what are you up to this morning?' he asks.

'There are a few things I'd like to find out. Firstly, why Rory thought turning up at the event was a good idea and where he went when he left. I want to know where he is staying and why he hasn't gone back to London yet. Hopefully the ANPR tracking on his car will shed some light. But for now, I'm trying to find out more about Ben. Like I said before, he had some weird preoccupation with Anna's death scene, to the point of obsession. I'd quite like a longer chat with him to find out where he was the night Anna died.'

Liam raps the table with his knuckles and offers to drive out to Ed's house later, to which I readily agree, already imagining half an hour when I can close my eyes.

Once he has left the room, I drain the rest of my lukewarm coffee and turn back to my computer screen. Ben had boldly stated to Reuben he was studying film making, but didn't disclose any more details. I assume because he was attending the event in Manchester, that he is also a student in the city.

Opening a new tab on my computer, I search for Manchester University film studies and peruse the list of websites, clicking on the one at the top. It is the homepage for the course with details about the modules to be studied, how to apply for the following academic year and information about various informal open evenings. I navigate the website for a few minutes and find a tab labelled 'media'.

When I click on this, I am confronted with a selection of short films contributed by this year's cohort. I scroll through the films and find that there are submissions from three different Bens.

I spend the next twenty minutes watching snippets of the films and, fairly easily, settle on Ben McCall as the one I met last night. Whilst the other two films edge towards the arty side of filmmaking, all hazy lights and slightly out of focus action, his veers towards demented. It features a park at night time and a fairly gory death, containing a masked man wielding a hammer.

As the masked man looks straight at the camera at the end of the film, my thoughts are drawn to my attacker. The darkness in his eyes cause my heart to skip a beat and my body gives an involuntary shudder, trying to rid the thought from my brain. I close the window and pull up another tab to search for details about Ed's second book, *A Violent Threat*.

From what I can gather, it appears the killer in the book commits many murders using his favoured weapon, a hammer. Now I understand the use of Hell Hammer as the second *Threat* film's adapted name, though I still think it is a woeful choice. I wonder if this short film is Ben's attempt at bettering Reuben, at showing his vision and his directing skills.

I click on the contact page and dial the telephone number provided. It rings for a few seconds before I'm connected to a pre-recorded message, stating that the office is closed for the weekend. I replace the handset and click on the email address, which opens a separate window on my browser. I type a short message, explaining my need to contact Ben and include my contact details before signing off and hitting send.

I spend a few more minutes trawling through the website in case there is any important information which I may have overlooked, before closing the browser window. As I stand up to leave my office, the phone rings.

'DI Erika Piper,' I answer.

'Hi,' the man's voice on the other line starts, 'my name is Professor McLeish, I have just received your email.'

I can hear the echo of our conversation and I assume he is using a hands-free kit. His tone is formal and I can't help but picture him as a stern man in robes, sat behind an ancient, oak desk holding a quilled pen between ink stained fingers.

'Thank you for getting back so quickly.'

'No problem. Emails ping straight to my phone and it sounded rather urgent. I'm actually heading into the office right now, I left in a hurry yesterday and I forgot my briefcase. I can spare a few minutes if it will help you.'

I assure him that a few minutes of his time would be very helpful and arrange to meet at the university campus in thirty minutes.

PROFESSOR MCLEISH'S OFFICE ISN'T what I expected. There is no ancient, oak desk. Instead, a flimsy metal desk houses a top of the range Apple Mac and a picture of two children, twin boys by the looks of it, judging by their matching clothes and hairstyles.

The desk sits in front of a huge window, overlooking the passing traffic on Oxford Road and framed pictures of iconic films including Casablanca and The Godfather fill the walls.

The man sat behind the desk doesn't match up with my imagination either; he's probably in his early forties, far from the old man I'd envisioned. Flecks of grey have spread through his thick, dark hair and his loose, casual clothes disguise an athletic body. He insists we call him by his forename, Derek.

'Sorry if I seemed a bit terse on the phone, Detective, even with the hands-free set up I don't like talking whilst driving.'

'Perfectly understandable,' I nod, 'it's a shame more people don't feel the same way.'

He smiles.

'I'm sorry to cut to the chase, but I have plans for today.'

He is sitting with his elbows on the desk, tapping his fingers together like a Bond villain.

'You said in your email that you required information about one of my students. Obviously, we have codes of confidentiality, but I'll see what I can do. Please, tell me what you would like to know.'

I tell him about my encounter with Ben the previous evening, and as my story wears on, Derek's expression changes to something nearing amusement. When I finish, he gives a little chuckle.

'I believe the student you are referring to is Ben McCall and that story sums up my experience of him so far. He is in his first year of the film studies course. He is very confident in his abilities, has ideas of grandeur and comes across as very,' he pauses, 'passionate.'

I smirk at the label and think back to my school reports when teachers would describe me as energetic when they actually meant I wouldn't sit in my seat for more than five minutes at a time. I'm guessing by 'passionate' he actually means 'a bit over the top'.

'Passionate is certainly one way to describe him,' I reply. 'I watched his short film this morning on the website; it didn't seem particularly in keeping with the rest of the films on there.'

The professor considers this. 'Yes, we did think long and hard about giving it an online platform, but in the end, who are we to censor someone's vision and creativity?'

'Don't you think it's over the top?'

'It's not my cup of tea,' he says, shrugging his shoulders, 'but then, if we all enjoyed the same thing, the world would be a boring place.'

'Has he ever mentioned *The Threat* books to you?'

He chuckles again. 'Of course he has, he wrote about them in his personal statement. He complained about how the film adaptation was terrible, and what he would've done differently. Before meeting him, I saw it as a young man who had very good critiquing abilities, a very important trait in someone who wishes to make films. Now that I have met him, I'd argue that it could come across as somewhat obsessive.'

The gut feeling I had about Ben is starting to intensify. 'Have you heard of the actor Anna Symons?' I ask him, changing my line of questioning.

'Yes, of course, I am the head of the film studies course after all,' he says. 'I was very sad to hear of her passing as I was a huge fan of the television series she was a part of. She made a very convincing detective.'

'And are you aware how she died?'

He replies in the affirmative. Before I can ask a follow up question, we are interrupted by Liam's ringing phone. He waves an apologetic hand, before rising from his seat and leaving the room. Derek shifts in his seat, perhaps thinking that Liam's departure is the opportune time to bring our meeting to a close.

'Derek, one last question, if I may?' I say, and he plants himself once more into his seat. 'Do you know the inspiration behind Ben's short?'

'I do,' he confirms. 'He came to me to ask if adapting a scene from a book was a copyright issue. I told him that since we weren't making them for profit, that it was OK to use the book without permission. He was so excited that he pulled the script out of his bag, there and then, and showed it to me. It was gory and, in my opinion, crass. I told him so and suggested he alter it, but it didn't deter him, I mean, you've seen the finished piece.'

My mind drifts back to the metal claw hammer being brought down mercilessly on the body again and again.

'Thank you for your time, professor. I don't suppose you have his current residence or a contact number?'

He contemplates this before turning on his computer. He quickly locates the information I have asked for and scrawls it on a Post-it note which he had retrieved from a drawer on his table. He hands it to me, leans across the table and shakes my hand, before getting to his feet.

As he moves around his desk to lead me to the door, Liam re-enters. He gives me a look that signifies he has news. When out of earshot, on our way back to the car, he shares the content of the phone call. Another body has been found.

14

'WHAT'D HE SAY?' Liam enquires as I lock the mobile phone and throw it onto my lap.

'He says he has no plans for tomorrow and to let him know when we are on our way.'

Liam nods and looks appreciative at Ed's flexibility. I tilt my head and rest it on the cold glass of the window, gazing with unfocussed eyes at the passing grey of the city centre buildings, preparing my mind for what's coming next.

I wonder what state the waiting body is in and if there is a link between this body and Anna's. The twinge in my gut tells me there is.

My thoughts turn to Anna's mutilated body, found on the ice only seven days ago. Such a waste of a life. I think about how many people her murder has affected; a loving family, a close group of friends and all those people who only knew her because of her films and glossy magazine covers, people she'd never met yet who still adored her.

Rory's appearance at the book event last night comes swimming into my mind and I begin to wonder what the purpose was. Is he genuinely a man grieving for his murdered fiancé who just wants an answer, a sense of closure? Or was it simply for show? Did he do it so that, if he is convicted somewhere down the line, he has this public performance as a reference point of his grief? A long sigh escapes my lips as we inch along with the rest of the city centre traffic.

As we pass the angular Crowne Plaza hotel, Liam slows to a crawl and tries to locate a suitable parking space, to no avail. A stationary car in a bay behind us suddenly indicates as if to leave and Liam, noticing this, waves in the air, inviting him to go around our car.

The man in the car raises his hand, thumb and forefinger almost touching, signifying a lack of space. Liam swears under his breath and takes off at speed, circling the hotel and, in no time, arrives back at the same spot where the car is creeping out of the space. Liam swears again and, when the car has just about vacated the bay, he manoeuvres in hastily, as if to show the man how it should be done. We are now a few streets from the waiting body. Liam locks the car with a beep and we walk down Shudehill towards the centre of the city.

Inviting smells drift from the open doors of greasy spoons on our left, all vying for custom on this cold December afternoon. My stomach rumbles, protesting at my seeming lack of interest in filling it. Sandwich boards narrow the pavement, forcing Liam and I to walk in single file. A huge, concrete ramp leading to a car park emerges on the other side of the road; a flimsy advertising board offers cheap parking for upcoming musical events at the Arena.

Arriving at a small pub on the corner of the street, we are greeted by a police cordon. Two men wearing waterproof coats, scarves and gloves approach us, introducing themselves as reporters from the city's newspapers. They attempt to ask us questions relating to the crime scene, which they know nothing about, judging from how general their questions are. Even though they are from competing news outlets, they seem very much a team.

Without a word to them, Liam and I flash our badges at the gatekeeper of the closed street and duck under the waist height blue and white plastic strip. When I look back at the two reporters, I see that one of the men has retrieved a flask from his bag and is filling a cup. It seems they are prepared for a long stay.

'Parasites,' says Liam, just loud enough for them to hear.

Ahead of us, on the kerb, are a number of white vans, affirming we have arrived at the designated location.

We sign in and accept the white, protective suits we have been handed. I struggle into mine, before tying my hair in a tight bun and pulling on a hairnet. Blue gloves and foot coverings complete the look. Liam takes a little longer to slip into his and when he is done, we approach a narrow alley at the back of the pub car park.

Martin, head of the Scene of Crime Officers, notices us. He says something to another suited man, before approaching us, shimmying under the police tape at the mouth of the alley.

'Piper,' he nods in my direction, 'Sutton.'

'What have we got?' asks Liam.

'Well, John's already had his fun with the body. He's just nipped to the office but he'll be back to talk you through what he's found. It's a mess. We've been here all morning and we're just finishing up, then it's your crime scene. Wait here a minute, I've got something that might interest you.'

With that, he turns and walks purposefully back into the depths of the alley before returning with an evidence bag in his hand. He holds it up so that I can see its contents; a single page that has been torn from a book. And I know which book.

'We might be in luck with this one. If you look here,' Martin says, pointing to the top left-hand corner of the page, 'there's a smudge. I reckon we've got at least a partial fingerprint here.'

He assures us that he'll put it through the system as soon as he can and let us know if it yields any results. He asks us to follow him and advances towards the alley again, though he stops at the entrance.

'If you look here,' he directs our attention to a patch of mud, 'you will notice two different shoe prints. One set belongs to the victim, we've matched the print against the shoes he is wearing, and the other is...'

'The same print as the one found on Anna's face,' I interrupt, finishing his sentence for him. 'So it's the same killer.'

'It is certainly very similar, stylistically, to the murder at the rink,' Martin agrees with a smile, before turning and marching back down the alleyway towards his team, leaving us to it.

Whilst waiting for John's return, I take a walk around the surrounding area.

The grimy pub at the entrance of the street is a small, red brick building with dirty, stained glass windows. The type of place where, I imagine, fights are commonplace. A sign above the front door, swinging in the wind, shows two silhouetted swans with necks intertwined and a blackboard attached to the wall advertises a Thursday night quiz with a meagre prize as well as regular weekend karaoke sessions.

Around the back, there are three cars in the pub car park; reluctant revellers who started the night with the best intentions before succumbing to the lure of intoxication. At least they were responsible and took a taxi home, no doubt with the aim of returning to collect them today, once the hangovers have subsided. A light drizzle has started to fall, so I shield my eyes in order to look skyward.

There are two CCTV cameras visible; one above a window on the back wall of the pub, pointing at the car park, the other angled towards the mouth of the street. I take my notepad out and make a note of the cars' number plates and to ask the pub owner for a copy of the CCTV tapes.

As I slip my pad back into the inside pocket of my coat, a silver Mondeo turns into the street and waits until the sentinel police officer holds the police tape high enough for him to pass under. It drives past us and turns into the pub's car park and, once stationary, John emerges from the driver's door. He spots Liam and me and raises his hand, before slamming the door and walking towards the alley.

'Hello, you two,' he says as we approach. 'Brace yourself for this one, it's quite a scene. Shall we?' He ducks under the police tape securing the alley and we follow suit.

The narrow alley is only accessible from this end, the other blocked off by a brick wall so high you'd need a ladder to scale it. This means that the killer must have left via the main road once the deed was done, walking past the pub and emerging onto the street, which CCTV should've picked up. The floor has been tarmacked, though a forest of waist-high weeds have found the cracks that offer them a chance of life and have claimed the alley as their home.

Colourful graffiti covers the walls, dull tags from years gone by melding with vibrant offerings from the new kids on the block. The stale smell of urine mixes with a faint whiff of iron, creating an overpowering stench. At the far end of the alley lies our victim. Dried blood on the ground forms a sinister, breadcrumb-like trail to the body.

At first glance, the position of his body could suggest he simply had too much to drink and has taken a tumble. He's face down on the tarmac with both arms stretched as far as they can beyond his head. He remains fully clothed and the only sign of foul play is the bloody mess that once was the back of his head.

From the man's bulk, I can hazard a pretty good guess at his identity. As we approach the body to discuss John's findings, Martin and his SOCO team leave the vicinity with a disconcertingly cheery goodbye, ready to try and make sense of the forensics found. When we are at the victim's side, John points to the head.

'I'm ruling this as a homicide,' he says, more out of duty than need, as it is clear that this was not self-inflicted, nor an accident.

He kneels down next to the body.

'As you can see, the most likely cause of death is blunt force trauma to the head. I'd say whoever did this has swung something pretty hard, perhaps a baseball bat or…'

'A hammer,' I interject, more a statement than a guess.

'Certainly a possibility,' John nods in agreement. 'Once I have got him back to the lab, I'll have a better chance of clarifying the murder weapon based on the impressions left behind.'

'Is there any other damage?'

'None apparent, though I haven't turned him over as I wanted you two to see the crime scene as the perpetrator intended.' I bend down to take a closer look, moving around the body to take it in from different angles, but aside from the head, the body does not look as if it has been otherwise harmed.

'Let's turn him, take a look and then he can be removed.'

We spend a few minutes deciding how the body is going to be turned with the aim of minimising loss of evidence and put our plan into place.

John positions himself by the head, Liam by the torso and I take my place by his legs. On the count of three, we all heave the body in the same direction, Liam doing the brunt of the lifting.

We take a step back and observe. My initial guess as to whom it is has been confirmed. Flat on his back, aside from a few injuries to his nose and mouth and without the bloodied back-of-the-head on show, you'd be forgiven for thinking he is simply asleep.

A glance at his torso, however, tells a different tale. His shirt has been ripped and a series of cuts and scratches are present on his enormous, exposed stomach. A similar story is told in the torn knees of his jeans. A lanyard with a picture of the deceased American pokes out of the pocket of his trousers.

'We've met this man before,' I say to John. 'He is an American film producer, known as Jay.' I fish the photo ID, issued from his production company, from his pocket and learn that his name was Jason Krist, an employee for one of the big Hollywood studios, judging by the logo in the top corner. I hand the ID to Liam who produces an evidence bag from his pocket and drops it in.

ID confirmed, I stand tall again and survey the scene as the killer has left it. I walk to the opening of the alleyway and look at the dried pool of blood on the floor before voicing my hypothesis.

'The pool of blood here,' I point, 'suggests that the victim was killed with a blow or blows to the head with a heavy object at this location. Jay was a huge man, tall and wide, and it would've taken a huge effort to get him down. Whoever swung the hammer… murder weapon,' I correct myself, 'must be around the same height as him, based on where the fatal injuries are.' John nods his agreement and the validation drives me onwards.

I take small steps towards the body, counting aloud as I go. I walk past the body and stop once I get to the point where his arms had extended to. Only then do I notice the men's incredulous, questioning expressions.

'The trail of blood and the cuts to his torso and knees suggest that the dead or dying body was dragged to this point from the entrance of the alleyway where I believe the initial attack took place. Fifteen small steps dragging a dead weight this size is not an easy task so I'd say the man we are looking for is at least six foot tall and either strong or very determined.'

I can think of a few who fit the bill.

15

ONCE THE BODY HAS been removed from the alley and the tent which was erected to preserve evidence has been packed away, Liam and I have one last look around. Liam moves some of the weeds aside and glances between the cracks before moving over to the bins at the end of the alley, lifting their lids and peering behind them.

Whilst he goes about his business, I take a seat on the low wall that separates the alley from the car park and take in the graffiti. Some of it is very intricate and would've taken a huge amount of time and effort; some has been scrawled on the wall by taggers who have vastly overestimated their artistic abilities. I've never understood why it's such a popular pursuit. Perhaps it is the need for humankind to stake a claim of ownership, to conquer, to leave a lasting mark. Perhaps it's just a bit of fun and I'm looking too deeply into it.

I scan the brick walls and one piece of graffiti catches my eye. It has been sprayed in vivid red paint that doesn't look completely dry. It's quite small and I can see why Martin may have missed it.

I hop up and walk over to the wall. The handwriting is messy, like it has been scrawled in a hurry. It has been written in capital letters and some of the paint has run down the wall joining a number of the letters together, creating the type of writing often found on t-shirts belonging to death metal bands.

Liam has noticed me staring at the wall so he walks over to see what has captured my attention and we spend a few moments looking at the writing which reads 'TICK TOCK.' I pull out my phone and take a picture of the writing.

'What do you reckon this means?' he asks.

At the minute, we can't even be sure that the killer has written this. It could be purely coincidental. However, if it was him, then this is a clear message with a less than clear meaning. Liam suggests that he could be telling us that we don't have long before he kills again. As we continue to hypothesise, a noise behind us brings our discussion to an end.

'Hi,' says a man, giving a small wave in our direction, 'I'm the landlord of the pub. I was the one who found the body this morning. A man who was here earlier said the detectives would probably like to speak to me.'

THE INSIDE OF THE pub does not match the exterior. The polished wooden bar running the length of one wall houses a number of pumps offering a choice of beers, both international and local, whilst a range of receptacles containing various spirits hang in front of a large mirror at the back of the bar. A fruit machine trills and flashes in a corner of the room and a number of identical tables and chairs fill the rest of the space. A door on the back wall conceals the stairs to the toilet upstairs.

'Not what you were expecting, eh?' says the man from outside, setting two steaming hot chocolates on the table for Liam and me. 'I love seeing the look on people's faces when they come in the doors expecting a cesspool only to be confronted with this!'

Ciaran, the landlord, is a short man with curly ginger hair. He's wearing the emerald rugby top of his national team and speaks very quickly. I think he has noticed my narrowed eyes, the concentration I'm exerting in trying to understand what he is saying, as he has slowed down considerably since we first met, ten minutes ago.

I thank him for the hot chocolate and take a small sip, burning the tip of my tongue slightly, before taking my recording device and setting it on the table.

'You mind?' I ask Ciaran. His bottom lip juts out and he shakes his head.

'Ciaran, for the purposes of the tape, can you confirm your identity?' He leans forward, as if being a few more inches nearer the tape is going to improve the clarity of the recording.

'Hello, I'm Ciaran O'Neill and I am the landlord of The Two Birds pub in Manchester,' he says and I suppress a giggle, imagining him as a contestant behind the sliding divide on Blind Date.

'Thank you. Have you been the landlord for long?'

He shakes his head. 'Not long, no. I bought this place... nearly two years ago,' he answers, after some thought. 'My wife and I have worked hard trying to change the image. It was a very much a pub for the 'rough' locals,' he raises his hands to make invisible inverted commas, 'but we didn't want that. We worked hard to weed out the troublemakers and ban them. Now, it's a safe place to come to.'

'And you were the one who found the body?' Liam asks.

He nods. 'I was out for an early morning cigarette,' he taps his lighter on the table. 'I've been trying to give up but, you know… Anyway, I was strolling around the car park having a cigarette when I noticed the blood at the entrance to the alley. I was annoyed 'cos we haven't had a fight in months, so I went inside to get a brush and some bleach to wash it away, and when I actually went down there, I saw… the body.'

As he finishes speaking, the door springs open and a man waltzes in, his hood pulled tight around his face. He scans behind the bar for any sign of life before turning and surveying the room. When he spots Ciaran, he gives him a thumbs up, though when Ciaran informs him that he is otherwise engaged and who we are, his face falls. He makes his excuses and vacates the premises.

'One of our regulars,' explains the owner, 'bit of a rascal.'

'Talk us through last night.' I say, trying to get back on track.

'It was quite eventful actually. Like I say, we've been working hard to change the perception of the place as well as the clientele. Last night started quite quiet for a Friday night. At about nine, a gigantic man with an American accent walked in, and propped himself up on a stool at the bar. He seemed pissed off at something so I left him to it. Drank like a fish, though it didn't seem to have much of an effect on him.'

I picture a stewing Jay walking into the pub after the event at the book shop. It was supposed to be a triumphant night, releasing details of his next big project, the conclusion of *The*

Threat trilogy, but instead it had been ruined by two guests who came with the intent of causing upset.

'After a while, as people tend to do with the lubrication of alcohol, he opened up a bit. He told me about a couple of assholes, his words,' he adds with a cheeky smile, 'who had annoyed him at some book thing he was at. I lent a sympathetic ear for a while but we started to get busy so I left him on his own. After a while, I noticed he was talking to someone and it was starting to get a bit heated. As I've said, we've worked hard to stop the fights and whatnot in here, so I wasn't having any of it. I went over to the guy, told him to leave and he did. Didn't put up much of a fight to be fair to him.'

'Can you describe the man he was arguing with?' I ask.

He closes his eyes.

'Aye, he was tall; I had to look up to see his face, though I'd have to say that about 90% of the population.'

He laughs self-deprecatingly.

'He had a patchy beard and was wearing a beanie hat,' he trails off and as I'm about to ask my next question, he adds, 'oh, and what looked like brand new boots. Those stood out because everything else that he was wearing seemed a bit old and tatty and those were clean as a whistle.'

The description of the man sounds very much like someone already known to us.

'Did the man seem homeless?'

He considers the question, appearing to be throwing the image of the man around his head. Eventually, he nods in the affirmative.

'Did you see where he went when he left?' I ask.

'I didn't sorry, I assume back towards Piccadilly Gardens in the centre, that's where most of them spend the night.'

'And what about the American?'

'He stayed for a few more pints, went to the toilet and then went outside to have a cigarette. Never came back. I figured, when I saw the size of the body this morning, that it was him.'

'Thank you, Ciaran, you've been so helpful. Just one last question.' He nods. 'Do your CCTV cameras work?'

'The one in here does,' he says, motioning to a black orb in the ceiling. 'The outside one facing the car park doesn't work but the one facing the street does.' I curse the CCTV gods; of course the most helpful one isn't working.

I paint a smile on. 'And is there any way you could send across the footage?'

He tells us that his wife is the technological one in their relationship and promises us that as soon as she is back from her shopping trip, he will get her to send it across, by tonight at the latest. We offer him money for the hot drinks but he declines, shaking our hands and showing us out onto the rainy street.

As we walk back to the car with hunched shoulders and our hands in our pockets, I can't help but speculate that this homeless man isn't homeless at all, and that he is the killer we desperately need to find.

16

'THEY'RE CALLING HIM *The Blood Ice Killer,'* DCI Bob shouts down the phone.

'Who?' I ask.

'The press. I've had someone from London on the phone and some fella from New York too.'

I think back to the reporters at the entrance to the alleyway and then the press conference from earlier where we confirmed the murder and appealed for witnesses. The press love a catchy moniker to capture the public's attention and to help sell their wares.

I suppose the fact that Jay is American has taken the case trans-Atlantic. I can see why he is so angry about it though. Now that it is in the psyche of the nation, we as a collective are going to be under so much public scrutiny.

Of course, DCI Bob has to answer to the commissioner, so I understand why he is getting his knickers in a twist. I assure him that the press will be bored by tomorrow and will have moved on. He barks a goodbye and hangs up.

I set the cutlery down with a clatter, push the empty plate away from me and take a sip from my wine glass, before grabbing my computer from the sideboard and setting it on the kitchen table in front of me.

The promised CCTV footage arrived in my inbox about an hour ago and has been downloading ever since; such is the vastness of the file size. It had pinged about five minutes ago to signify the task had been completed and was ready for viewing. I open the downloaded folder and look at the two files included, before double clicking on '*Interior 1*'.

A separate window opens and shows silent black and white footage of the inside of the pub I had visited earlier in the day. I often wonder how they can collect coloured, high definition images of the surface of Mars, but haven't managed to transfer that picture quality to CCTV cameras here on Earth; I know where they would be more useful.

The video is nearly two hours long, the time at the bottom corner of the screen showing 9:06 p.m. when I press play. As Ciaran told us earlier, the pub is quite empty for a Friday night, a few casually dressed drinkers loiter by the bar, drinks in hand, whilst a group of friends mill around the pool table. A man laughs heartily as his opponent scuffs his shot, sending the white ball soaring into the air and dashing across the floor.

A few minutes later, Jay; alive and well, enters the pub and props himself on a stool, which looks like it is struggling under his weight, at the bar.

The video shows the night playing out exactly as Ciaran said it had. Jay says something to the barman, who pours a pint and leaves it to settle, before presenting it to the American a few minutes later. Ciaran appears to attempt to engage Jay in conversation but judging from his body language, he doesn't reciprocate. Ciaran looks a tad nervous and wanders off, leaving Jay alone.

For a long time, Jay sits there, draining drink after drink before seemingly becoming more sociable and engaging in conversation with Ciaran. The bar has filled steadily and Ciaran is leaning in close to Jay, presumably to hear him over the din of the punters. The barman then ends the chat and goes to serve waiting clientele. Then our man of interest appears.

Dressed in the same outfit as when he was captured on CCTV on the night Anna died, he sidles straight up to the American and begins to talk. Jay looks at him for a few seconds, a flicker of recognition flashing across his face, and quickly becomes agitated.

With a swift movement, belying his bulk, he rises from his seat and closes the gap between himself and his unwanted guest just as Ciaran intervenes and the homeless man is banished. The time stamp now shows 10:32 p.m.

Jay looks like he is considering going after the homeless man and makes a start for the door. He pauses after two steps and seemingly thinks better of it because he sits down again and orders another drink. He speaks to the barman for a little while longer and once he has drained his glass, staggers towards the stairs in the direction of the toilet and leaves the bar at 10:59p.m. The video ends with nothing new gleaned, save for a time frame of events.

I click the red box and exit the video, before entering the folder and opening the file labelled *Exterior 1*. Again, the video starts at 9:06 p.m. and as in the first, a few minutes after the video starts, Jay enters the frame.

He marches up the street with his head down, before pulling back the door to the pub and entering. A tall, shadowy figure, dressed in dark, non-descript clothes appears in the frame not long after, grabs the handle of the pub door, takes a peek inside, thinks better of it and scuttles down the alley at the side of the building. *Could this be the killer?*

His clothes don't match the homeless man who appeared in the video I've just watched, so now we have two people of interest who have sought Jay out on the night he was murdered.

Nothing of note happens for a time; a number of people enter the pub, though far more merrymakers ignore it completely, searching instead for a livelier atmosphere deeper into the trendy Northern Quarter.

At just before half past ten, the homeless man staggers up to the door with his pronounced limp and pulls it open at the second attempt. He reappears a few minutes later and leans against the pub wall. His chest seems to be rising and falling at a rate of knots, perhaps his encounter with Jay has caused a spike of adrenaline.

He then proceeds to do something I did not expect; he pulls the front of his trousers down and holds his penis in his hand. A group of women wearing sashes, presumably on a hen do, dash across the road, as though alarmed by his actions as he stumbles towards the kerb.

The homeless man makes his way down the alley, penis still exposed. I assume he needs to relieve himself, perhaps that's why he entered the pub in the first place, simply to go to the toilet. Though, judging from the video and how he made a beeline for Jay upon entering the pub, he seemed to know that the American film producer was there, which makes the toilet theory seem a little naïve.

At 10:59 pm, Jay staggers out of the pub and fishes a box of cigarettes from his jacket pocket. He leans against the wall of the pub for a minute or two, attempting to shield the lighter's flame from the wind, before turning around and peering into the darkness of the alley. Something seems to have piqued his interest. He throws his unlit cigarette to the floor and stamps on it, before wandering into the alley towards the source of the noise.

At 11:16 p.m. the homeless man, presumably having committed the dastardly deed, scurries out of the alley, turning left before picking up speed and hobbling as fast as he can towards the town centre. Interestingly, he is hatless. He can't have lost it during the attack, because Martin would've found it whilst sweeping the alleyway for forensic clues, which makes me think the attacker must've stowed it in his bag.

This footage is invaluable as it gives us a massive clue which could make all the difference to the case; there is not a hair on his head. The light from the moon bounces off his bald head as he exits the frame.

My gaze drops from the screen and I consider what I've just watched and how important this video may prove to be. We now have a time of death and a prime suspect with a number of very distinguishing features. My musing is interrupted by a flash of movement on the screen. Another figure is exiting the alley, a lot slower than the homeless man.

I'd forgotten about the mysterious, hooded figure that had entered the alley over an hour ago. He has pulled his hood down and it is now resting on his shoulders, his bushy hair exposed. Just as he approaches the pub door, he wanders into a pool of light which illuminates his face. He seems to notice this and glances up at the streetlight, then pulls his hood up again and sets off at pace, in the opposite direction to the homeless man. I rewind the video, pause it on the image of his face and my eyes widen in disbelief.

17

'YOU'RE SURE IT WAS BEN?' Liam asks, pressing the indicator down.

'100%' I reply. I've spent the journey to Ed's house describing, in detail, my findings from the CCTV footage received from the pub. He waits for a number of cars to pass, before pulling across the road and into the quiet cul-de-sac in the west of the city.

He crawls along, seeking out house numbers, using the controls on the wheel to lower the volume of the radio, as if the noise level could somehow affect the performance of his eyes. The houses that line the street are extravagant and spacious, mostly two storey red brick structures with sloped rooves and at least one garage, though most have a sports car or an upmarket 4x4 parked on their driveway. A few modern constructions have appeared on some plots, the kind you'd watch visionaries assemble from state-of-the-art materials on Grand Designs, much to the annoyance of the owners of the more traditional abodes.

'Sounds like we need a chat with the filmmaker prodigy,' says Liam, echoing my own thoughts.

A huge, pebble-dashed house at the end of the street bears the number forty-two - Ed's house. Liam pulls up on the street at the bottom of a steep driveway, which leads to a double garage and a wide, rose red front door flanked by stone pillars. The elevated position of the house in relation to the end of the street lends it a rather regal quality.

'How the other half live, eh?' I say, as we climb out of the car and begin our ascent up the driveway, edging past a sleek sports car which seems to impress Liam.

Reaching the top, I disregard the doorbell and, instead, rap the hard wood three times. After a minute or so, there is movement in the house before the door opens, revealing a bleary-eyed Ed. Dark rings under his eyes make it look like he hasn't slept in a week. His hair looks different from the other night at the book shop, though I can't quite put my finger on why.

He picks up an oversized hoodie that was hanging over the bannister and throws it on, pulling the hood over his head. Baggy jogging bottoms, torn at the bottom, trail on the floor, covering his bare feet. He stares at us for a few seconds before recognition slowly spreads across his face.

'Shit, sorry... yeah,' he mutters, rubbing the sleep out of his eyes. 'Come in, come in.'

He opens the door wide and Liam and I step over the threshold, removing our shoes and setting them on a mat just inside the door.

He shuffles ahead of us, down the wide hallway and enters a room on the right. We follow him into the living room, where he has thrown himself onto a leather sofa, leaving two matching chairs for Liam and me.

The room is sparsely decorated; a huge flat-screen television is mounted above a marble fireplace which has a number of trophies from literary events placed upon it, an overflowing bookshelf takes pride of place along the back wall and a small drinks cabinet serves as a table in the middle of the room.

He takes our drinks order and works his way out of the deep sofa with a soft groan and leaves the room. When he returns a few minutes later, he hands me an overly milky tea and Liam a small glass of water, before easing himself back onto the sofa. 'So, officers, how can I be of service?' he smiles.

'Can you run us through the night of Anna's death?'

'Straight to the point,' he nods. 'Well, Reuben and I decided to meet in Altrincham to do a bit of preparation on our, as it turned out, doomed event. He lives there and I live close by, so it made sense. We needed to sort a running order and write a basic script. So we met in a bar, did a bit of work, and then Anna showed up with her friend. Her friend didn't stay long because she pulled some guy and left, so Anna joined us at our table. Reuben didn't seem too pleased; they had a bit of history you see? Which I assume you know about.'

Neither Liam nor I respond, so he continues.

'She got drunk pretty quickly so we decided to get her home. Unfortunately, she couldn't verbalise where she lived so Reuben said he'd take her to a hotel. I offered to help but he said he was fine so I got a bus back here.'

His recount of the night matches the action played out on the CCTV images.

'And the next day, you travelled to Scotland for a writing retreat, is that correct?'

He rubs his hand on the back of his neck and takes a deep breath.

'That was the plan, but sadly I didn't feel up to it. My bags were packed and I was excited to see some old friends, but instead I couldn't get out of bed for a few days. I knew we had these events coming up so I was trying to recover.'

'What was it?' I ask.

'The flu, I think. I just kept being sick and had a high temperature. Luckily, it had mostly passed in time for the event, though I still don't feel back to my best.'

'Can anyone verify this?' I enquire.

He shakes his head.

'Single, sadly,' he says with a melancholic smile. I make a note to find any way to verify his version of events. Up until now, I hadn't considered him as a suspect, but this new revelation that he was in the area and not ensconced in the Scottish Highlands rules him very much in.

'Did you know Anna personally?' Liam asks.

Ed pushes himself out of the sofa again and walks over to the window, pulls the blinds to omit the oppressive rays of sunlight and stands leaning against the marble fireplace. The hoodie he is wearing is at least two sizes too large, and I wonder if he was once the correct size for the garment and has subsequently lost a lot of weight or if he simply prefers the comfort of loose clothing.

'Not personally, no.' He pauses and unleashes a volley of coughs.

He holds his hand up in apology and shuffles back over to the sofa, picking up his water and taking a few small sips.

'Professionally, yes. You see, before I became a full-time author, I was a make-up artist, mostly on fashion shoots for magazines but occasionally on film sets. When I sold the film rights to my first book, the deal was enough that I could give up the make-up gig and I did for a while, but to be honest, I kinda missed it. When the filming started on *Blood Ice*,' he grimaces, 'I was on set anyway, as a producer and I helped out occasionally in the make-up department, just for fun. On the days when Anna was on set, I helped apply some of her prosthetics and we got on well. But that's as far as I knew her and after I was thrown off set, I never saw her again until she turned up at Limas.'

'Thrown off set?'

Ed looks like he wishes he hadn't let that little nugget of information slip. 'Not thrown off, per se. Asked to leave.'

'Asked?'

'Told. Told quite firmly actually, by Jay. You probably saw him at the book event; the huge, loudmouth American. He said I was getting too big for my boots, interfering when I saw that they had changed something from the book. Told me it was, and I quote, *a fucking adaptation* and that I had no say in the creative process.'

He barks a hollow laugh which turns into a series of coughs and rubs his eyes.

'Wasn't just me, either,' he continues. 'He walked around the set like he was Jesus Christ. I swear Jason Krist isn't his actual real name, he probably changed it to make it closer to the Almighty's. He threw Anna's boyfriend at the time, can't remember his name, off the set too. Said he was proving to be a distraction, that Anna wasn't fully focussed or giving her all.'

'So you and Jay didn't get on?'

He smiles.

'Understatement of the year. We hate each other; have done ever since *Blood Ice*. He screwed me royally on my film deal. Like I said before, it was enough for me to give up the day job. But it wasn't a good deal. I thought he was looking out for me, but he knew what he was doing and I was very green. Too trusting and excitable. Then to have me thrown off the set, it was embarrassing. Jay laughed in Reuben's face when he asked him if I could come for a set visit on...' he pauses, gulps and a flash of fury spreads momentarily across his face, 'the second film. I refuse to call it... what they've ended up calling it.'

'Do you blame Jay for ruining the film versions of your books?'

He nods.

'Jay was the man with the money and with the final say. It's his fault it turned out so shit. God knows what he has done with the second one.'

His breathing has become laboured and his face has become a shade of crimson. I let the venom settle before informing him about Jay's fate. His eyes widen and his nostrils flare, his mouth opens trying to find words but only succeeds in releasing a quiet gasp. I imagine he's wondering if, after revealing his loathing of Jay, he has said a little bit too much.

'Poor bloke,' he says, putting his hands over his mouth and bowing his head. 'However much we didn't see eye to eye, no one deserves to go like that.'

'Pages from your books have been left at the crime scenes. One from *The Threat* at the ice rink where Anna's body was found and one from *The Violent Threat* in the alleyway where Jason's body was found. Do you know anything about this?'

Genuine confusion flashes across his face.

'Are you accusing me of these murders?' he asks.

'We're not accusing you of anything. We're simply asking if you know why this might be happening?'

'I don't know anything about it. It makes me feel sick that whoever is doing this is using my books for ideas. Maybe someone is trying to frame me…' he trails off, seemingly aghast at the prospect.

We allow him a few moments of silent reflection before I ask if I can go to the toilet. Ed nods and gives me directions to the bathroom. I stand up and walk out of the room and into the hallway. The stairs are made from heavy wood and my shoeless feet slip on the polished oak.

I walk across the carpeted landing, which is decorated with framed pictures of Ed alongside people who I assume are famous, judging from their attire, but whom I do not recognise. The bathroom, at the far end of the hall, is half tiled, half painted. It has a sterile feel. A bath fills one corner of the room, and a luxurious shower with body jets occupies another wall.

After relieving myself, and having washed my hands, I glance in the mirror of the cabinet above the sink and re-tie my hair into a ponytail. When I'm done, I notice that the cabinet is padlocked. I pull the padlock which results in a loud clanking of metal on metal, but the cabinet remains firmly shut. I wonder why anyone would lock their own bathroom cabinet. I'd get it if it was lower to the ground and there were children roaming about, but a single man locking a bathroom cabinet seems suspicious.

I take my phone out and snap a picture of the rectangular box on the wall. I slip my phone back into my pocket and leave the bathroom, closing the door behind me.

On the way back towards the stairs, I notice one of the doors is slightly ajar. The drone of conversation drifts up the stairs, though I still peer over the banister to make sure no one is in the hall below, before pushing the door gently.

The hinges emit a squeak that seems to echo around the house and I curse under my breath. The murmurs from downstairs cease and I stand unmoving, as still as a statue, waiting for something to happen.

After a few seconds which seem like a lifetime, the talking resumes and I exhale, realising I'd been holding my breath. I poke my head around the door and survey the scene. The bedroom of the bachelor is not what I'd expected at all; the room would not look out of place in a five-star hotel.

The bed is covered in pristine white sheets, immaculately made without a single fold in the material. A comfortable fabric sofa rests against a wall. A small round table sits beside it with a closed laptop and a notebook perched atop. Shirtsleeves spill out of the mahogany wardrobe's slightly opened doors and a range of moisturisers and aftershaves rest upon a set of matching drawers.

I'm about to leave when I spot something that appears massively out of the ordinary for such a carefully decorated room. A plastic mannequin head lies on its side on the floor, as if it has fallen off the nearby bedside table. Soulless eyes stare in my direction, and I can barely contain a chuckle at the deep red lipstick and slanted eyebrows that have been drawn on, giving it an angry countenance.

My mind runs wild thinking about the possible explanations as to why the head is in the house at all, let alone in his bedroom. Perhaps it's what he uses to test and perfect his make-up skills on, given what we've just learned about his previous occupation. Perhaps it's something a little more… perverse?

With one last peek around the room, and one last curious glance at the mannequin head, I pull the door closed slowly, coughing to mask the screech before making my way downstairs.

'We were about to send a search party!' smirks Ed upon my reappearance.

'Sorry, tummy problems…' I reply, rubbing my stomach as if to emphasise the point. Ed looks suitably disgusted and does not offer any further remarks.

'What's with the lock on the bathroom cabinet?' I ask, trying to sound casual.

'My mother has been diagnosed with cancer recently,' he says sadly, to which we offer our condolences. 'I insist that she stays here at least once a week so that I can keep an eye on her and she keeps some of her medication in the cabinet. I can't bear thinking about it, and every time I open the cabinet, it's there, you know? So I lock it, and only open it when she's here. Out of sight, out of mind, as they say.'

His last sentence is barely audible and ends in a sob which gets caught in his throat. He tries to regain his composure, looking up at us with a smile, though his eyes appear slightly wet.

'Ed, thank you so much for having us and for answering our questions. It has been very helpful. We just have one more, and then we'll be out of your hair.'

Liam unzips the bag that has been lying at his feet and pulls out a manila folder. He leafs through the contents until he finds what he needs, removing a single sheet of paper and handing it to Ed. 'Do you recognise this man?'

Ed studies the picture on the piece of paper before handing it back to Liam.

'It's the kid from the book event that gave Reuben shit, isn't it? He had a hat on that night as I recall, I didn't recognise him.'

'Didn't recognise him?' I repeat. 'Have you seen him before?'

He nods. 'His hair is pretty recognisable, like that guitarist from Guns 'N' Roses. Yeah, he was the guy that Anna's friend got off with in the bar in Altrincham, the night Anna was murdered.'

18

THE SAT-NAV CONFIRMS that we have reached our destination. Liam pulls into a marked space at the side of the street and we exit the car, gazing at one of the buildings used to accommodate the students of Manchester University.

The ugly rectangular block stretches high into the cloudy sky, the grey concrete punctuated at regular intervals with small porthole-style windows. The street is quiet, the lashing rain discouraging any al fresco socialising.

With our jackets pulled over our heads, we run across the street and into the building, stopping at the reception desk, which is being manned by a portly security guard with wispy hair who watches the water dripping from our clothes onto the floor with a hint of displeasure. On his desk, a small, artificial Christmas tree with twinkling white, fibre optic lights attempts to inject some colour into the drab surroundings of the lobby.

We flash our police IDs at him and he studies them before enquiring if he can help. We explain the reason behind our visit and he waves us through, informing us that the lifts are currently out of order. I grimace as I re-read the address the professor has given us for Ben's ninth floor residence. Reluctantly, we resign ourselves to the stairs.

The interior of the stairwell reminds me of one belonging to a city centre car park. The stench of stale urine infiltrates my nose, and we have to kick our way through burger boxes and fast food wrappers. Small amounts of graffiti decorate the walls, mobile numbers displayed with flirtatious messages alongside the ubiquitous ejaculating penis.

Considering this block is currently housing future doctors and teachers amongst other professions, I can't help but snigger at the immaturity of it all. With burning calves and protesting lungs, we finally make it to floor nine and let ourselves into the narrow hallway.

The ninth floor contains multiple doors with peeling paint and metal numbers screwed into them. We make our way along the stained laminate flooring until we reach the door marked 909 at the far end of the hallway. I rap my knuckles on the door twice and wait, but there is no answer.

I knock again and place my ear on the door, straining to hear any movement but there is not a sound to be heard.

We knock on a few more doors as we make our way back down the hallway to no avail. Perhaps the students have already left for the Christmas holidays or they are simply holed up in a pub, living the stereotypical student life. Either way, it's been a wasted trip. With a resigned sigh, we make our way back down the stairs, bid farewell to the man at reception and stride out into the driving rain towards the patrol vehicle.

As we climb into the car, a group of five students appear around the corner at the end of the street, laughing and pushing each other playfully. They are appropriately dressed for the weather, raincoats with hoods pulled up against the unrelenting downpour.

One of the group – a boy dressed in a khaki raincoat and dark jeans – notices the police car and freezes on the spot, the grin slipping off his face. Long, curly hair escapes his hood and blows in the wind. It's Ben.

As I begin to remove myself from the car, he glances around the street and casts a guilty look at his friends before plucking the cigarette from between his lips and launching it onto the ground and disappearing around the corner of the building at pace.

Without thinking, I immediately sprint in the same direction, much to the bewilderment of the group he has just left. I catch sight of him at the end of the street, his hood has fallen and his distinctive curly hair is bouncing in time with each step.

He crosses the street without checking if the road is clear and a car has to slam on its brakes to avoid colliding with him, the honking of the horn and the volley of insults aimed in his direction fully justified. I lose and regain sight of him a number of times as I chase him through side streets and past rows of terraced houses.

His long legs propel him along the street with ease and I struggle to keep up, but as we career towards the city centre, the crowds of weekend shoppers slow his progress. Luckily, his stretched frame and wild hair are distinctive amongst the throng of people and I keep my eyes fully locked on him as he approaches the Arndale shopping centre.

Just as he reaches the doors, a large group of shoppers with bags full of Christmas presents exit, blocking the doorway. Leading with his shoulder, he barges through the group and into the shopping centre, nearly knocking two unfortunate women to the floor.

The women are still in the doorway, gesticulating angrily towards the rogue student. This delays my entry and by the time I have navigated the obstruction, Ben is out of sight. Standing in the middle of the ground floor, I gaze through shop windows trying to catch a glimpse of his bushy hair but he is nowhere to be seen.

'Fuck,' I mutter, bending over and resting my hands on my thighs, feeling the lactic acid settle into my tired muscles, just as an out of breath Liam appears by my side.

We spend over half an hour patrolling the shopping centre, Liam having ascended the escalators and me on the ground floor, scouring the place for our missing student, though with no sign of him, we concede defeat and trudge back through the rain towards the student accommodation.

Liam unlocks the car and, as I am about to get in, I hear someone shouting, as if to attract my attention. I look for the source of the noise and find a young man with his hood up and scarf pulled tight around his neck, waving at me from the outdoor smoking area of a pub across the road. He stubs his cigarette out in an ashtray, turns around to knock on the window of the pub and mouths something through the glass.

A minute later, the rest of the group who had accompanied Ben around the corner of the street a little over an hour earlier emerge. One of the girls sucks the rest of her brightly coloured drink through a straw and sets the empty glass on one of the tables. They make their way sheepishly across the road towards us.

'We want to know if we can help,' says one of the girls, before inviting us into their halls of residence.

We ascend the stairs again, thankfully only to the fourth floor, and enter the room of a boy called Jamie. The students stand awkwardly against the wall, forming what looks like an impromptu identity parade.

Imploring them to relax, which they don't and who can blame them; they have just seen us chase their friend through the streets of the city, we begin our questioning.

The consensus is that Ben is a good friend and passionate about his craft, though one of the girls who is called either Libby or Lizzy; I can't tell as she is mumbling, does admit that when he's drunk, he becomes a bit creepy and weird. The others shoot her a look as if she is betraying their friend, though she doesn't seem to notice.

Having gleaned all we can, we leave the room and make our way downstairs to the reception area. We provide Greg, the man at reception, with a picture of Ben and insist that he call us as soon as he returns, to which he readily agrees.

Once back in the car, I sink into my seat, exhausted from the day, my thoughts drifting to a chilled glass of wine.

But first, a debrief with DCI Bob Lovatt. Great.

'OUTSMARTED BY A STUDENT, EH?' smirks Charlotte. We are sitting in the newly opened cocktail bar in the precinct of Marple. The new proprietors have opted for a Hawaiian themed interior, the wood panelled walls covered in framed prints of sandy beaches and beautiful sunsets. A rubber palm tree, not quite fully inflated, is languishing against the brick wall at the back and a cheerful cover version of a well-known pop song plays through the speakers at an unobtrusive volume.

Despite the array of cocktails listed on the chalk boards behind the bar, we've opted for two large glasses of red wine, much to the derision of the bearded bartender in the brightly coloured floral shirt.

'I don't know about being outsmarted. Out-ran, definitely,' I reply, taking a sip of the Pinot Noir.

'Either way, it amounts to you doing a shit job!' That fucking smirk again. If it was anyone else but Charlotte goading me, I'd be pissed off. But because it's delivered with her trademark comic effect, I can't help but laugh, even if it impinging on the truth.

'The day did get better though,' I inform her, pulling a brown envelope out of my handbag and wafting it in her face. She tries to snatch it from me, but my reflexes are too quick and I pull it out of her reach to safety, nearly knocking my wine glass over in the process.

Ripping open the seal, I pull out the A4 piece of paper and unfold it. 'Ready?' I clear my throat and read the note aloud;

To DI Piper, I'm truly sorry for wasting your time. Please accept these by way of an apology. Reuben.

I look up at her and am greeted with a deeply unimpressed face. I know she hates suspense, so I leave the remaining contents of the envelope a mystery for a few more seconds until she looks truly venomous and my bravery falters. I set the two matte black tickets on the table. Each piece of card is decorated with a crimson border and an outline of a claw hammer. Embossed words detail the time, location and dress code for the premiere of *Hell Hammer*, the second film in *The Threat* film trilogy.

'Wow!' she perks up, having spent a few minutes studying the tickets, 'I really liked the first film! Girls' night out! Thanks, Erika.' She starts reeling off her clothing options; the red, sparkly dress is disregarded as it is far too low cut, the purple dress she wore to the Christmas party last year has shrunk in the wash and now reveals most of her bum-cheeks, so that's no good either. Just as she is proposing a girly shopping trip, she pauses when she registers the expression on my face.

'This isn't for me, is it?' she asks, to which I scrunch up my nose and shake my head, all the while grovelling apologies. 'Who the fuck would you rather take than me?'

I realise at this point that I haven't told her about what happened last time we were out together. About Tom. For the next few minutes, I divulge every sordid detail about my night with Tom, knowing this will win her round. Her mood changes as she asks question after question, and once she is content that no detail has been spared, she confirms that taking Tom sounds like a good idea.

I pocket the tickets and the conversation moves on to more mundane subjects; her new hair which she hates because the stylist didn't layer it properly and her sexy weekend away with her husband. We each have one more drink and call it a night.

I SPIN THE HOT water tap with my toe and let the water run, topping up the bath I've been sitting in for just under thirty minutes. I glance at my hands and realise they've gone wrinkly, immediately thinking of Macauley Culkin in the bath in *Home Alone*, feeling super creepy in the process. I blow out the candle that has been illuminating the room and grab a towel from the radiator, pulling it around me, enjoying the continued warmth.

Once I'm mostly dry, I lie down on the bed and grab my laptop from the top drawer of the bedside table. A beeping noise signals a low battery, so I retrieve the charger and plug it into the wall before logging in.

I access my work files and load up the CCTV footage from the bar on the night Anna was killed. I watch again as Anna and her friend enter the bar, the action playing out in the exact same way as on the first viewing. Except this time, my attention is not trained on Anna, but on the friend. She is a little shorter than Anna, dressed in a plunging, stripy playsuit with her dark hair pulled into a high ponytail. As Anna is accosted by fans, her friend stands to the side, hand on hip with more than a hint of jealousy on her face.

Anna reconvenes with her friend and they go to the bar with a small crowd following them, smartphones in hand trying to get a picture of the celebrity in their midst. Once they've been served, they shimmy to the dancefloor where they remain for the duration of a few songs until Anna glances up and finds Ed and Reuben at the back of the bar. She leans close to her friend and says something in her ear before leaving the dancefloor.

Amongst the crowd, I spot Ben's bushy hair bobbing along to the rhythm of the music. I watch as he moves towards Anna's friend who has stayed on the dancefloor, sipping on her drink and swaying to the music.

Ben approaches her and they begin to dance, bodies becoming closer until he puts his hand on the back of her head and leans in, pressing his lips to hers. After a few minutes, he pulls away and they smile at each other. The friend motions for Ben to follow her, and they make their way, fingers intertwined, towards the table containing the director, author and actor.

Amicable words are exchanged between Anna and her friend whilst Ben hangs a few steps back, presumably a bit star struck at being in the presence of one of his favourite authors. The friend and Ben then leave the bar via the front door, probably retreating to one of their houses.

As the video finishes, DCI Bob's final words from the briefing echo around my head; it's time to get to the bottom of this.

19

I STAND IN FRONT of the door for a minute or so, gathering my thoughts. Over the years, I've been to hundreds of bereaved families who have been mourning the loss of their loved one, but it never gets any easier. Today, it's the turn of the Symons family. Their sadness, a few weeks on, may have become tangible to them, perhaps almost understandable, and here I am, ready to unstitch the healing wound grief had so callously inflicted.

I puff out my cheeks and press the doorbell, grimacing at the catchy jingle at odds with the reason of my visit. A woman with dark brown hair and greying roots, styled in a bob, pulls the door back and peers out from behind it. Her eyes flicker to our badges before closing, mentally preparing herself for the next hour. Long eyelashes and plump lips lend her a glamorous appearance; her thin body agile, as if she has tried to stave off the ageing process by keeping as fit as possible.

She introduces herself as Linda, Anna's mother, and then wordlessly summons us in. We step over the threshold and Liam bends down and begins untying his laces.

'Don't worry about your shoes, love,' she says, waving us on to follow her through the hall and into the room on the left.

The living room is decorated in natural tones; ivory walls, charcoal carpet, a black corduroy corner sofa. A pine sideboard sits against one wall; the end door slightly ajar as paper tries to escape the confines of the cupboard. A matching television stand is positioned in the corner of the room.

'Can I get you anything? Tea? Coffee?' she asks.

We place our orders and she retreats to the solitude of the kitchen where I can hear her as she goes about her business; the rush of the water as she fills the kettle and the clattering of crockery.

While she is absent from the room, I have a look around. Framed photographs, mainly of her daughter, line the walls at eye level; a young Anna treading the boards in a primary school play, perhaps where she fell in love with the thespian lifestyle. Another photo shows teenage Anna with her mother and father, posing near the edge of the Grand Canyon. The final photo shows adult Anna, posing in a flowing, blue ball gown, thrusting an award towards the camera with a look of pride on her face.

The tinkle of china announces Linda's return to the room. She shuffles in carrying a tray containing three willow-patterned mugs, which she sets on the glass table in the middle of the room before distributing the drinks from a matching teapot.

I set mine on the table so that it can cool and take a seat on the sofa beside Liam, whilst our host sinks into the chair opposite. Now that I get a good look at her, I can see that her thin body doesn't look fit after all. She looks emaciated, probably down to not eating for the past few weeks. Her bones protrude from under stretched, pale skin. Dark rings under her eyes signal that she probably hasn't slept very much in the recent past either.

'Have you found him yet?' she asks with a sigh, though she almost certainly knows the answer already.

'Not yet, but that's why we're here,' I answer.

'I'll do whatever I can to help,' she replies, reaching for the box of tissues on the floor beside her chair and dabbing under her eyes.

'I know you have already been through this with our colleagues, but we appreciate anything you can tell us,' Liam smiles. I take out a notepad and a pen, pulling the lid off with my teeth.

'Can you tell us about Anna's visit to Manchester?'

Linda looks confused. 'I've already told the police about this.'

I nod. 'I understand, but it would be very helpful to hear it first-hand.'

She takes a deep breath, readying herself once again to delve into her despair.

'Well, her boyfriend was going away on business for a week or so, so she thought she'd come up and spend some time with me. Since her father died a few years ago, I've been on my own and haven't seen a lot of her, she's been so busy. We had a lovely few days, she treated me to a day at the spa; champagne, full body massage, the works... it was magic. On the last night,' she suppresses a sob, 'she was on the phone to Rory, that's her man, and they had a bit of an argument. They've had their ups and downs over the years. Anyway, once she'd hung up, she phoned a friend and then went upstairs to get ready to go out. As she left the house, she told me not to wait up and hugged me. That was the last time I saw her alive.'

The sobbing starts in earnest now and tears begin to flow down her cheeks. We give her a few minutes to get it out, nodding our sympathies when she glances our way.

'Sorry about that,' she whispers, looking slightly embarrassed.

'Don't be silly,' I reply, before pressing on. 'Linda, the reason we are here today is because we have some new information, we have been tracking Rory's car. He has passed a traffic camera around this area a number of times, and we were wondering have you had any contact with him?'

She nods.

'Yes, since Stan passed away, the house has gone into a bit of disrepair. After what happened with, with Anna,' she stammers, 'Rory got in touch to ask if he could come round and visit. When he was here, he offered to do a bit of DIY, fix a few bits. I was happy for him to do it, of course, and it was nice to have company, someone who loved Anna the same way I did.'

'Did he stay here?'

'No, I did offer, but he said he was staying in the city.'

'Did he say where?'

She shakes her head.

'He always seemed quite private, so I didn't ask him. The only thing he said was that he had some business to attend to.'

I glance at Liam. The fact we know that he hasn't returned to London for work casts a massive question mark over his head. And what business was he referring to? Actual business?

Or murder? We need to find him as soon as possible to find out.

'Linda, was Rory ever violent with Anna?' I ask.

'Only once that I know of, but she said they were both drunk,' she adds, rushing to his defence. 'They were very much in love, and he's a lovely man. They were about to get married.' She suddenly looks angry. 'You don't think he has got anything to do with it, do you?'

'At this stage, we can't rule anything out. Can you remember when he was last here?'

She thinks for a minute, mouthing the days. 'Probably three or four days ago, he was supposed to finish up the garden. He'd just about done fixing the shed, but said he had broken a wrench and misplaced his hammer. He nipped out to get some new tools, and never came back. Every time I phone him, it goes straight to his voicemail.'

His hammer.

My professional mask slips and I can't help but think what she must be going through; in the space of a few years she has lost her husband and now her only child has been murdered. Her world must feel like it's been turned upside down, and now we've been pulled into her orbit and implied that the man she thought loved her daughter could be the man who wielded the blade.

I think about my own sorrow, about the overwhelming possibility of not being able to have children and consider for the first time that maybe it's actually a blessing in disguise - the world can be a cruel place.

I'm brought back into the present by the sound of Linda blowing her nose, her puffy red eyes surveying the room, avoiding ours.

'Do you mind if we look around Anna's room?'

She shrugs her shoulders half-heartedly.

'Of course. But the police have already been through her room, left it in a right state too. They took her laptop and some other things, they said they'd return them but they've not been brought back yet.'

We leave the room and ascend the stairs, my hand gliding up the recently painted banister, the faint smell of fumes wafting towards my nose. Maybe Rory is innocent and really did have business to attend to in the north and simply wanted to do something helpful, wanted to be close to someone who understood the pain he was feeling.

Anna's room is the first on the left at the top of the stairs. The door opens, revealing a dark space - a pair of floor length black-out curtains are pulled tight across the window, preventing any light from entering. A musty smell leaks out, indicating that, aside from the police's intrusion, the room has remained untouched since Anna was last here. I walk over to the curtains and pull them to the side, allowing a wash of light to invade the darkness.

It's a large bedroom, painted a light purple, filled with many of Anna's belongings, which is strange considering her life was being lived in London. Evidence of Anna's final trip here is littered around; the straighteners resting on a ceramic plate on the floor beside a full length mirror, an open suitcase overflowing with clothes, as if they have been cast out in a hurry whilst searching for an appropriate outfit for what turned out to be her last night out.

Signs of Anna's earlier life are here too. A bookcase filled with novels aimed at teenagers and shelves dedicated to medals and trophies, engraved in the early 2000s, probably from her final years in primary school. Posters from films she has appeared in adorn the walls, some framed and some not. Her doting mother downstairs who has kept this shrine to her daughter was, is, obviously very proud of her.

My mind wanders to my dad, in a similar position to Linda, now that my mother is no longer with us. I think of him on his own in the expanse of his house and make a mental note to visit him as soon as I can.

It's obvious that the police have been here and have given it the once over. It has the feel of a room that has been gone through with a clinical and unemotional feel, taken apart and reassembled again with dispassionate hands, oblivious to the life, the girl, who used to live her life within the four walls.

Liam and I spend some time poring over the room, pulling out desk drawers and poking through the contents, but there is nothing of note between the notepads and biros with little ink remaining.

We check the usual spots that are good for hiding things you want to keep hidden; under the bed, behind furniture and in drawers stuffed with clothes, but to no avail. Our task is made harder by the fact we don't even know what we are looking for, or if there is even something to be found. But I have that feeling in the pit of my stomach that there is something to be uncovered in this room.

Frustrated and sweaty from the effort of the search, I take a seat on the bed and cast my eyes around the room. The brightly coloured film posters that line the room are varied in genre. Anna was seemingly a very talented actor and appeared in films ranging from period pieces to sci-fi epics. The framed posters are hung in regular intervals and are uniform in size. Except one.

The poster for *Blood Ice* is enclosed in a box frame that juts out roughly two inches from the wall. The frame, unlike the rest, has recently been moved. A layer of dust that has settled on the other posters has been disturbed on this frame; finger marks show that this frame has been of interest to someone recently. The frame also hangs at a slight angle.

I stand on the bed and unhook the frame, setting it face down on the bed. Small, metal teeth hold a backboard in place, to stop the poster from falling out. I dig my fingernails underneath each one and pull them vertical, and when the final one has been moved, the wooden backboard slips easily out of place.

A faded envelope is nestled behind the picture, stowed away from prying eyes. No-one but Anna was ever supposed to see this. I have an uneasy feeling as I peel back the flap and I can hear Liam's breath quicken as he strains to get a good look over my shoulder as a card is revealed.

A pencil-thin woman is lying on a hospital bed, her leg held aloft and wrapped in a cast. She is looking angrily at a man who is slouched apologetically by her side. A speech bubble from the injured woman's mouth says 'Next time, just say good luck!'

I laugh at the good-natured card, obviously intended for Anna as she prepared for an audition, a new job, a big moment in her career. My laugh is cut short as I open the card and read the seven-word message scrawled inside.

One day, you'll get what you deserve.

20

DCI BOB FIDDLES WITH his tie as he welcomes and introduces the new officers in the room. The case, now with two murders and no progress on catching the killer, has been allocated more resources; more bodies, more feet on the street. He finishes his spiel, before giving me a nod that tells me it's my turn in the spotlight.

As I make my way to the front of the room, I have a flashback to the last time I was in this position, almost three weeks ago on my first day back. My palms were sweaty and my tongue felt swollen and huge in my mouth. But today, I feel like a new woman. Or rather, that I've returned to the woman I once was.

I bend over the computer and open the folder I need, double-clicking on the PowerPoint icon. The file loads and appears for everyone to see on the big screen. Three faces stare out at the team in the room. I give them time to take them in before pointing at the young man with the wild, curly hair and patchy beard.

'Let's start with Ben,' I say to the assembled officers, taking things back to basics for the new eyes present.

'Ben is a film student who loves *The Threat* books but didn't like the films, nor Reuben or Jay for bringing them into the world. When we went to question him yesterday, he ran away from us and we lost him in the city centre. Obviously, he has something to hide. We have someone watching his student accommodation around the clock with instruction to apprehend if possible.'

As I'm about to move on to the next suspect, DCI Bob stands up.

'We don't seriously think that this boy,' he points to the screen, 'would kill two people just because he doesn't like a film, do we?'

A smattering of sniggers sound around the room and I can see why he thinks it's ridiculous.

'I know it sounds a bit over the top, but he also told me that he has fantasised about re-creating Anna's murder scene from the first film. He claims that he could've done a far better job than Reuben managed to. He has also made a short film which has been published on the university website depicting graphic violence in which the killer uses a hammer, much like the death of…'

'…Jason Krist.' DCI Bob finishes my sentence and takes his seat, apparently happy with my considered response. I focus the laser beam from my pointer on Ed's face.

'This is Ed, the author of *The Threat* books. Initially, we thought he was on his way to the Scottish Highlands at the time of Anna's murder but that has been disproven. CCTV footage shows him getting on a bus and leaving the area where Anna was murdered, a good chunk of time before her death is believed to have occurred. We have reason to believe they had a relationship, a non-romantic one, but they were still known to one another. Pages from his books have been recovered from the murder scenes. When we informed him of this, he seemed genuinely upset that he may have an indirect hand in the killings. I don't see him as a suspect.'

Bums are starting to shuffle in seats and the room is becoming hot and stuffy. It reminds me of assembly in primary school, sitting on the dusty wooden floor, my bony bottom in agony because of the prolonged lectures from the head teacher. I am now that head teacher. I plough on, speaking a little faster for the benefit of my class.

'Finally, Rory,' I say, motioning to his handsome face on the projector screen. 'Rory is Anna's fiancé, who claims he was away on business when she was murdered. We've been tracking his car for the past week or so and know that he has been at Anna's mum's house. When we went there, she claimed he had been there to help out with some DIY. He disappeared without saying goodbye the day before Jay's murder. There has not been a sighting of his car since, which leads us to believe that he is either using a different vehicle or relying on public transport. His company in London have confirmed that he has not returned to work. He may have returned to the capital, but we believe he is still in the area. It is imperative that we find him.'

I close the PowerPoint to illustrate that the briefing is finished. Class is dismissed. The room empties as I eject my USB from the computer but when I look around, DCI Bob is lingering by the doorway.

He closes the door and looks through the small window, seemingly making sure there are no eavesdroppers. The creases in his forehead and the slightly sweaty demeanour imply that whatever he is about to say isn't good. As he adjusts his tie again, I brace myself.

'There's no easy way to say this,' he begins, and I can feel my stomach summersault. 'My wife has been diagnosed with cancer.' His chin drops onto his chest and I can see tears glimmer in the corner of his eyes. I don't know if I should hug him or if this would cross a professional line. Instead, I reach out and give his shoulder a little rub.

'I'm so sorry. Is there anything I can do?'

'Actually, there is,' he replies, rubbing his eyes. 'Would you mind taking charge of the investigation for the next week or so? I've been given compassionate leave and I know we are neck deep into this, but I can't be here at the minute, I can't focus on anything else but her. I need to be with Janine. I realise that you haven't been back long, but I trust the case will be in good hands with you.'

I assure him that I'm more than happy to take the lead and he thanks me before opening the door and leaving the room. I check my watch and realise that if I don't get a move on, I'm going to be late for Jay's final appointment.

LIAM AND I JOG through the sliding doors of Manchester Royal Infirmary and make our way down the corridor towards the morgue. John Kirrane, forensic pathologist, sits just outside the door of the mortuary in his overalls and socks, waiting for us with a polystyrene cup of coffee.

He brushes our apologies for being late away with a wave of his hand, before pressing the ID card hanging from his lanyard against an electronic box on the wall, which emits a beep and frees the locked door, letting us into his place of work.

On the other side of the door, Jay's body waits. The clean, antiseptic smell of the room fills my nostrils and my eyes water at its strength. Trevor, John's trusty technician, emerges from a side office, greets us and hands us a set of overalls each which we pull on.

'How's the case going?' John asks, slipping his feet into a pair of mortuary boots.

'So so,' I reply, filling him in on our suspects and our lack of a breakthrough.

'Maybe this man can help,' he says, pointing at Jay.

His body is lying on a gurney in the middle of the room, the shimmering metal at odds to the greying body lying upon it.

'Let's get started, shall we?' John says to no-one is particular.

He walks to a small control panel built into the workbench at the side of the room, and presses a button. A green light appears, indicating that the microphone suspended from the ceiling is now recording.

John begins by stating the name of the victim, followed by the date and time of the post mortem. He then spends a few minutes walking around the body, verbally recording what he can see.

Once the preliminary observations are recorded, Trevor and John carefully remove Jay's clothes and place them in clear, plastic bags, to which Trevor affixes a label. John then circles the gurney once more, making more notes about the naked body.

A spotlight in the ceiling just above the body reveals everything, everything about his life and everything about his death. Translucent scars from misadventures suffered years ago gleam in the light, divulging the climax to stories I'll never know the start of. Dark hair covers the majority of his torso and legs, black against the paleness of his cold body.

I take a step back, realising that I am in Trevor's way. He circles the body with a video camera whilst John carefully measures each and every abrasion present on the deceased's body, all the while documenting his findings aloud.

Once John is happy that nothing has been missed on the exterior of the body, he begins the autopsy. I don't consider myself squeamish, but the sights, sounds and smells experienced during the examination leave nothing to the imagination and I long to be outside, gulping in fresh air.

'Well, I think we can safely say that cause of death is blunt force trauma to the head, inflicted by an instrument likely to be a hammer. The indents in the back of the cranium indicate such.'

He gives a nod my way and beckons us over to the top of the gurney for a clearer look at Jay's head.

'Now, I say indents in the back of the head because there are a number of them; five in total. I imagine one blow from behind took him to his knees and another took him to the floor. They are well centred blows which would suggest that the victim didn't hear the attacker approach.'

John points to Jay's face.

'The third, fourth and fifth blows came when the victim was face down on the ground. The blows were delivered with such force that it cracked the skull and caused this damage,' he says, indicating the swollen, likely broken nose and the chipped teeth visible behind the lips. 'In my opinion, he would've been dead by the third blow.'

John points out a few more details and finishes with the body, leaving it to the mortuary assistants to clean and close up again. He takes off his gloves and walks into the office at the side of the room. Liam and I follow him, wiggling out of our suits as we go.

John taps a few keys on his computer and the screen comes to life. 'I'll have a full report ready soon, but judging from where the points of contact are and taking into account the considerable size of the victim, I'd say that your attacker is a tall man, at least 6 feet tall. I'd also say that he is reasonably strong, considering how far he dragged the body down the alley. He looks up from his desk with a grim smile. 'I hope that, for now, that is enough to go on.'

I assure him that it is, though the profile fits all three of our suspects and doesn't narrow the field any. I glance at the clock on the wall and realise for the second time today that unless I get moving, I'm going to be late. After all, it's not every day one gets to attend a premiere for a Hollywood film.

21

NO MATTER HOW MANY times I drag the brush through my hair, the knots refuse to shift. Acknowledging the fact that no amount of brushing is going to untangle the mess, I pull a bobble from a drawer and tie my hair into a high ponytail, pulling it tight. Knowing that I don't have long before Tom picks me up, I apply a little make up and laugh at the absurdity of it all.

I imagine the long-legged, buxom-chested beauties in their flowing, designer dresses and perfectly coiffed hair, swanning elegantly around the foyer of the cinema, champagne in hand, having spent the day relaxing and getting ready at their leisure. And then I turn up with my messy hair, sparse make up and cobbled-together-at-the-last-minute, borrowed-from-my-pregnant-sister dress.

Still, I console myself with the knowledge that none of these women will have spent the day in a room watching a body being cut open and medically examined. I apply some lipstick before making the decision that it makes me appear washed out, and remove it immediately.

As I'm squeezing the toothpaste out of its tube, the doorbell rings, signalling Tom's arrival. I move the toothbrush into the flowing water, before plunging it into my mouth and walking down the stairs. I open the door and let Tom in, holding the toothbrush up to show that I can't speak, and point to the sofa. I run back upstairs and spit out the minty paste, cursing myself as a small white stain settles into the boob area of my dress. Great. If I were a superstitious woman, I'd say all signs point to tonight not turning out well.

Tom is standing near the door with a bunch of flowers. Coming down the stairs towards him reminds me of the scene from Titanic where Leonardo DiCaprio turns to greet Kate Winslet with a wide smile. Except Tom does not look like a third-class passenger aboard a doomed ship, he looks suave and sophisticated.

He is wearing a black three-piece suit with a bow tie and a pair of pointed, shiny shoes. His hair is short and smart and he's clean-shaven. I point to the space between his nose and lip, where the trendy moustache once sat proudly. He shakes his head sadly.

'DCI Bob had a word with me about it. Apparently, I had to get rid of it because of health and safety. Bob is worried that someone might grab it if I was trying to apprehend them. I tried to just make it a bit smaller, but it's still too soon to attempt Hitler-chic,' he explains, with a smile.

I laugh and he tells me I look beautiful, before giving me a kiss on the lips which causes my heart to hammer hard against my ribs. I turn the lights off in the house, lock the door and he leads me to his car, opening the door for me in very chivalrous fashion.

As we roll along the crowded motorway, we discuss the case, amongst other things. Tom decides that tonight should be a night to switch off from work and to simply enjoy a night not thinking about crime, aside from what happens on the silver screen.

Twenty-five minutes later, we pull into the Trafford Centre car park, which is, as usual, full to the brim. We coast through row after row of cars before cutting our losses and opting for the large overflow car park, as far away from the building as it is possible to be, which means a longer walk. At least it's not raining.

We begin our walk down the concourse towards the Odeon cinema. In the rush of getting ready, I'd forgotten that the premiere was taking place on a cold winter's night in northern England, and had not had the foresight to bring any warm clothing. Noticing my shivering body and chattering teeth, Tom removes his jacket and insists I wear it, draping it over my shoulders. I thank him for his thoughtfulness and we proceed towards the cinema.

'Did you watch *Blood Ice*?' he asks. Tom had lent me the DVD of the first film in the series last week and insisted I watch it before tonight, as some of the characters make a return in the film we are here to see tonight, *Hell Hammer*.

'I did,' I confirm.

'And?'

I hold my hand horizontally and give it a wobble. 'It was OK. I think I would've enjoyed it a lot more had I not been privy to seeing Anna's actual semi-decapitated body.'

'Fair play,' he nods, 'that probably does take away some of the mystique.'

'And Ben, the student,' I add, noticing his quizzical look, 'does have a point, her death scene in the film looked a bit… amateur.'

THE USUALLY BOG-STANDARD cinema foyer I've been in a million times has had a major facelift. Gone are the cardboard cut-outs advertising upcoming films, gone are the groups of tracksuit wearing teens and gone are the usual bored looking staff that seem like they'd rather be anywhere else.

Instead, the place has been transformed into a setting fit for Hollywood royalty. Black, fabric drapes displaying a red claw hammer, much like the one found on the Soviet Union flag; its handle emblazoned with the letters HH in thick, block capitals, hang from the ceiling. Those same letters have been stitched onto the backs of the waiter's waistcoats, a team of whom are currently moving around the room, silently offering guests a selection of costly alcohol.

A selection of well-groomed and expensively dressed individuals mingle in the foyer, huddled around in little groups. The majority have their phones out, taking selfies and live streaming their evening to their social media followers. It makes me yearn for a simpler time, before phones were glued to hands and having fun was more important than the illusion of having fun. I often hark back to the days of my Motorola Timeport with fondness, to a time when sending a text message was considered a novelty. God, I'm getting old.

Tom and I spend some time trying to identify any film stars. We wander around the foyer and he points out a few faces I vaguely recognise and reels off some films they've starred in. I'm amazed at how much detail he remembers and make a mental note to invite him to the next pub quiz I go to.

Just then, our attention is drawn to a commotion near the area by the escalators. Ed, the author of *The Threat* series, the man I recently paid a visit to, has arrived to some fanfare. A few people gather around him and pleasantries are exchanged, hands shook.

It seems that Ed is on the road to recovery. The dark rings underneath his eyes have disappeared and his skin emits a healthy glow. Gone is the deathly pallor from when we saw him last. Gone too is the oversized hoodie and tatty pyjama bottoms, replaced instead by a fitted three-piece suit and a silk bowtie.

With a smile that looks painted on, he makes his way through the crowd, pausing for some photographs before casting a sideways glance in our direction. He takes another step and does a double take, studying my face and seemingly reaching the realisation of who I am. His brow furrows as confusion flashes across his face. He changes course and approaches us, holding out his hand which I take in mine. His palm is sweaty.

'Inspector, you had me at a disadvantage for a moment there.' He lets go of my hand and I pull it behind my back, rubbing it on my dress to get rid of the dampness.

'Mr Bennett, how are you?'

'I'm getting there,' he says, coughing into a handkerchief he has produced from an inside pocket of his jacket. 'Still not fully recovered from the illness that kept me from the trip to

Scotland and if it weren't for the fact that this is Reuben's night, I wouldn't be here.'

I'm surprised. 'Even though it's the film adaptation of your book? This is your night too, surely?'

He waves the suggestion away with his hand. 'Did you see the first film? It's no more an adaptation than a complete re-write. That film had none of my DNA and I doubt this one will either. Still, as I say, tonight is all about Reuben and his vision. I may not like the film but I love him like a brother and that's more important.' His gaze drifts towards Tom.

'Ah, sorry,' I say, forgetting I hadn't performed introductions, 'this is Tom.'

'Pleasure to meet you, pal,' Tom says, 'I'm a fan of your work.'

'Husband?' Ed asks with a smile whilst shaking Tom's hand.

'Boyfriend,' Tom answers, looking from me to Ed, though it sounds more like a question than a statement. The silence hangs in the air for a few seconds too long, taking us into awkward territory.

'Nice to meet you, mate,' Ed says, glancing at his watch. 'Well, I think the film is starting soon, so I best be heading in. I hope you enjoy it,' he says, before bidding us goodbye and walking away towards the cinema doors.

I FOLD THE RED, velvety seat down and sink into it, placing my drink into the holder attached to the arm-rest and shoving a handful of popcorn into my mouth. The room is nearly at capacity and is buzzing with excited chatter. A curly haired man and a woman wearing heavy make-up near us are discussing the trailer and who they think the killer is.

For the first time, I'm hit by the fact that the upcoming film is going to feature a killer who murders people in the same way Jay was killed and I feel slightly uneasy. Silence descends in the room as the lights dim and a man I recognise from a rom-com walks onto a small stage at the front of the room, positioned just in front of the screen. His pinstriped suit is expertly tailored to his athletic frame and his long hair hangs loosely on his shoulders. He picks up a microphone from a table at the side of the stage and waves to the room, which erupts with applause.

The man, who Tom tells me is the actor who plays the newly-promoted detective in the film, smiles at the warm welcome and once it has subsided, raises the microphone to his lips.

'Can you hear me?' he asks the room, and receives a chorus of affirmations in reply. 'You'll have to forgive the loose nature of my introduction. Our wonderful director, Reuben Amaro…' the room bursts into a round of applause which the actor encourages by raising his hand to his ear.

He waits for the clapping to subside before continuing.

'Reuben was supposed to be doing this bit but, alas, he has not yet arrived. Although, knowing him, he is plotting some form of elaborate entrance.'

He looks to the rafters and, without the microphone, shouts, 'If you're up there Reuben, now's the time to come down.' Once more, the room fills with laughter. The assembled crowd are in good spirits and the feeling is contagious. Even though it seems like an in-joke, I can't help but smile.

Once the mirth in the room has again abated, the actor on the stage takes on a more serious tone.

'On a night of celebration – and it is a night of celebration because it truly is a wonderful film – we must not forget the heartbreak we have suffered. I'm talking, of course, about the tragic death of Mr Jason Krist. Without him, none of us would be here tonight. This film, along with *Blood Ice*, were his babies and we all owe him a massive thank you for letting us be a part of his passion. I'd ask you please to observe a minute of silence in his honour.'

The room collectively bows its head and the minute's silence is impeccably observed. Once completed, the actor signs off by saying he hopes we enjoy the film.

He walks off to another rapturous round of applause and takes his seat near the front of the room, pretending to wipe his brow much to the amusement of the woman in the seat next to him.

Tom reaches for my hand and grasps it, pulling it onto the arm rest and intertwines his fingers with mine. The few lights that had remained on for the presentation now fade to black and the velvet curtains covering the screen slowly begin to open.

The beam of light from the projector bisects the room and the silver screen flickers to life. There is a collective gasp in the room as the first image appears.

It is Reuben's face.

It is covered in blood.

22

AN EERIE SILENCE FILLS the room, punctuated only by Reuben's ragged breathing. Everyone has edged forward a few inches in their seats, waiting to see what will happen next.

For a few seconds, Reuben simply stares at the camera. His face fills the entire screen. It's as if the film has been paused. The terrible violence he has been subjected to is evident on his face. His nose has ballooned in size and is surely broken; blood streams from both nostrils and the area under his eyes has turned purple. His forehead is covered in vicious, raised welts and chunks of skin are missing from his cheeks and chin. He looks terrified.

After what seems like an eternity of silence, he clears his throat. It echoes around the room and takes the audience by surprise, causing most of the people present to jump with shock, like a perverse Mexican wave. His bloody lips smack together and he begins to speak, his voice gravelly.

'Hello,' he mutters into the camera and then stops. His eyes flit around the area behind the camera, before coming to a stop and focussing on something. Or someone. He pleads silently for a few seconds before he regains some of his composure and fixes his stare back on the camera lens.

Watching his face; his expressions, I begin to wonder if this is all a publicity stunt. The actor who introduced the film in lieu of Reuben hinted that the director was a fan of a grand entrance. Perhaps this is it. Perhaps we're going to watch him pretend to be kidnapped and suddenly he will appear here in the cinema, sitting amongst us.

'Sorry I can't be there tonight,' he mutters, 'but I'm a bit tied up.'

His eyes move from side to side like a typewriter, as if reading from some form of script. This could be a clue that the whole thing is staged, what genuine kidnapping has a script? Maybe the trauma to his face is purely a fantastic make-up job.

The camera slowly pulls away from Reuben's face and his body comes into view. A thick rope is tied around his neck and knotted at the side. The remaining rope leaves the top of the screen and must be connected to something above him, out of shot. He is topless and his slightly doughy torso shows signs that it too has been subjected to the same treatment as his face. He is still wearing his trousers, though they are stained with blood and dirt. The camera stops zooming out once it reaches his knees.

As the angle widens, the huge expanse of a room is exposed. The room is dimly lit; the huge glass windows, grey with dust, forbidding any outside light. The brickwork, caked in dirt and grime from years of toil within the room, appears black.

It reminds me of a scene from Sin City - the vivid red blood on Reuben's face and the gold belt buckle glinting in the small amount of light emanating from the strip lights overhead the only colours discernible amid the dull background. As I take in the scene, my heart thumps in my chest and my breathing speeds up. The room is reminiscent of the one I had my encounter with my attacker in; the shadowy corners and the threat of death bring back terrible memories.

Reuben's voice brings me back to the present with a jolt. As he continues his monologue, I gaze around the cinema at the faces illuminated by the screen. Most are staring at the screen, expressionless, confused and appalled at what they are watching. Some have physically turned their bodies away, unable to watch the unfolding of the film. A minority are staring up at the projector's booth, shouting for the projectionist to put a stop to this.

My attention is brought firmly back to the screen at the sound of a voice from behind the camera. There is no-one else on screen so I assume that the voice belongs to whoever is controlling the camera, the man in charge of this heinous filth. I curse myself that I didn't hear what the man said, because from the look on Reuben's face, it means that things could be about to escalate. He pleads with the invisible man. He grovels. He swears on his life that he hasn't committed whatever crime has been levelled against him.

Tom gets up from his seat and whispers that he will be back soon, before slipping past the rest of the people in our row and disappearing down the faintly lit steps and out of the double doors.

I notice Ed a few rows in front, in a seat at the end of the line. I can see his body trembling and he looks like he's about to be sick. I'm now certain that the video is not a fake, as Ed is clearly distressed. I feel so sorry for him, having to watch his friend be treated like this.

On screen, the camera zooms out again. Reuben's feet appear, standing on an upturned plastic crate, the type pubs use to transport and store bottled beer. The end of the rope is now visible and is attached to a set of railings above him, hanging with a little slack.

Suddenly, there is a cry of anger and Reuben's pleas are cut short as the crate he is standing on is kicked away, with only a boot visible. No other part of the perpetrator's body enters the screen. The slack in the rope tightens and Reuben is suspended in mid-air, his feet swaying just inches from the ground, from safety.

His cries and guttural gasps for air fill the room as his hands pry at the rope which has tightened around his neck. His eyes are as wide as I've ever seen another humans and I watch in horror as the poor guy fights for his life. The audience are now leaving in droves, some have been physically sick and the smell of vomit is filling the room. Some are frozen in their seats as if unable to move even if they wanted to, staring incredulously at the screen.

Within a minute, Reuben has lost consciousness and his body simply hangs there. His face has become blotchy and the whites of his open eyes have filled with blood. Though unconscious, his dangling body jerks; his ribcage is still moving, still trying to take in air, fighting to stave off death.

But alas, to no avail. Within another minute, it's clear that Reuben's body has lost the fight and has surrendered to the Grim Reaper.

23

POLICE TAPE HAS BEEN rolled across the area housing the self-service ticket machines, separating the cinema from the eateries on the top floor of the Trafford Centre. Uniformed officers are stationed at the bottom of the escalators, just inside the tape, in an attempt to placate the members of the public who have pre-paid for their tickets and have turned up expecting to be entertained by the latest blockbuster, only to be turned away.

Just up the steps, in the circular foyer of the cinema, a large group of people remains. The cinema staff are gathered behind the ticket counter, gossiping amongst themselves, having not seen the film but relying on overheard information. Most of the premiere attendees have left, unaware they were going to be needed to give a police statement.

Some of the guests who left early are mingling with those who stayed, listening to them recount the grisly ending. Others are happy to stand by themselves, assuming the worst outcome without needing confirmation. Police officers walk around the room, taking statements, though it's an almost pointless task as it's not the crime scene and it's almost certain that no-one will have any useful information. Still, as DCI Bob always says, it's best to cover all bases.

Meanwhile, Tom and I are upstairs in the projectionist's booth. Once the film of Reuben's demise ended, the trailers had started and the film looked set to carry on as it should've.

When Tom had left the auditorium, he'd climbed the stairs and waited outside the room we are sat in now, in anticipation of the projectionist doing a runner. However, he had remained steadfastly in his booth and Tom had only entered when I had joined him and insisted he stop the film.

The projectionist is a young man in his early twenties. He appears to be stuck in the nineties; his Oasis-inspired hair style - long at the sides with a fringe cut straight across his forehead is paired with a retro Smiths T-shirt.

The man is clearly very proud of the musical output of his hometown. Skinny jeans and a pair of scuffed, red Adidas trainers complete his look. I imagine he would be donning a green parka if the room wasn't so cramped and sweltering hot. He introduces himself as Neil.

'Tell us how this happened,' states Tom.

'What d'ya mean?' Neil replies in his thick Mancunian accent.

'I mean, how the fuck did a snuff movie make it onto the screen?' Tom retorts, his voice raised.

'A snuff movie?' Neil repeats, looking bemused. 'No, you don't honestly think that was real, do you?'

'You don't?

Neil shakes his head so fast that it is in danger of snapping off his neck and swinging into orbit.

'Not at all, he's known for this kind of stuff. He's always pulling pranks and making films like this. Seriously, a lot of them are on YouTube, you should look them up. My favourite is the one where he drives off a cliff.'

He laughs at the memory of the film but stops abruptly when he sees our faces.

'The crowd didn't seem to think that it was fake, how are you so sure it is?' I ask, and for the first time he turns to me and studies me intently.

His dark brown eyes rake me up and down, and I notice that his cool, calm demeanour might be an act, as I notice the beads of sweat on his forehead, though that could be down to the humidity in the room.

'I'm a film student and last year, one of the modules we had to do was marketing. It was pretty much a study of his publicity campaigns. Honestly, he does this kind of thing all the time.'

He stands up and pulls a laptop out of a drawer. I look at it enquiringly and he explains that when he has set the film up on the projector, he uses that time to work. He sits down again and opens the lid of the laptop. His fingers glide over the buttons and he looks pointedly at the screen with his tongue poking out between his front teeth. He taps a few more times and then turns the laptop around so that Tom and I can see it.

'And this is…?' Tom says.

'This is a list of all the things Reuben has done for a bit of publicity, specifically during promotion for a film or TV show he has been involved in. He's been doing it since his debut film. My tutor sent us this to help with our essay on marketing, and how Reuben used this technique so effectively.'

I take the laptop from him and have a look at the list. It is a humorous list, and proves that Reuben has had good ideas to cause a bit of a stir in order to promote his work. But most of these are funny, light hearted ideas designed to capture the public's imagination. They are certainly not in keeping with a strangulation video.

'Where do you study?' I ask, handing the laptop back to Neil.

'Manchester Uni.'

'You don't happen to know a Ben McCall by any chance?' I take a stab in the dark and a look of confusion flashes across his face.

'Yeah, I do actually. We're not friends or anything, but I know him to see. He is in the year below me. How do you know Ben?'

'What do you know about him?' I ask, answering his question with a question.

'Not much, like I said, he's in the year below me so our paths don't really cross, though I know there is a fair bit of notoriety about him. Apparently he has submitted a few controversial shorts and has been threatened with expulsion. I've heard he has sort of crossed the line with regards to violence and gore and the tutors are getting a bit sick of it.'

I cast a sideways glance at Tom and underline Ben's name in my notebook.

'Thanks for your time, Neil. Whether this is a fake or not, we are going to need to take the film in order to examine it. Has anyone else had access to it prior to you?'

'Only the delivery man, but it's been under lock and key since I signed for it yesterday. It's not every day we get to hold a premiere here, especially for a film by a director I love. It's a shame he didn't turn up in the end,' he adds as he begins moving around the room, boxing up the film paraphernalia and handing it to us. I speak into my walkie-talkie and ask for assistance in tagging them and bringing them down to the cars.

I make my way back down the stairs towards the foyer, leaving Tom to supervise the collection of evidence and to make sure that Neil doesn't tamper with anything.

The crowd has now thinned and there is less of a police presence. I sit down on a bench near the entrance to the miniature golf course and reflect on the craziness of the evening.

I'm still convinced that the film was real and that Reuben is no longer with us, but Neil's insistence on the contrary and expertise on the matter are niggling at me. Perhaps it *is* all a set-up; a publicity stunt and I have fallen for it hook, line and sinker.

I search through my bag and take out my phone, navigating through the phonebook until I find Reuben's phone number. Then I hit dial. To my surprise, it rings, though no one answers and eventually the call ends, with no option to leave a message on his voicemail. I re-enter my phonebook and scroll through the list of names until I find the one I'm looking for - Ross Powell.

Ross Powell is a computer whizz who works in the digital department of the police. What he doesn't know about all things digital isn't worth knowing. Even though it's quite late, he answers within a few rings, his voice bright. There is loud gunfire in the background and I assume he is watching an action film.

'Erika, it's been a while!' he says. 'I assume this isn't a personal call?'

I explain the reason for my call to him whilst he munches on something, the crunching noise making its way through from the other end of the phone. I want the film transferred to DVD format and I want the sound enhanced. He doesn't respond immediately, I assume he is finishing chewing, but when he does, he utters two syllables.

'Easy.'

We arrange delivery of the film for first thing tomorrow, once they have been examined by forensics, and he tells me it won't take too long and that I should have them by the afternoon. We exchange goodbyes and I hang up.

Before I stow my phone away, I notice that there is a text message waiting to be read. I open my inbox and note that the message has been sent from Reuben's phone. My heart drops. I've ruined his night by closing down the cinema, fooled by the realism of the prank. I imagine the news has got back to him already and he's pissed off.

When I open the text message, the phone nearly drops out of my hand. Attached is a picture of Reuben's dead body. It has been removed from the noose and laid on the dirty, concrete floor. His eyes are closed and the imprinted ligature marks around his neck are fresh and raw.

Aside from the horrific injuries he has had inflicted on him, he looks almost peaceful. As I study his bruised and battered face, a second text appears, its arrival heralded by a loud beep that scares the life out of me. It contains ten words from the same number:

COME AND FIND ME, ERIKA PIPER. TIME IS RUNNING OUT

24

'SHIT, SO HE'S MAKING it personal,' says Angela.

We've been discussing the text message sent from Reuben's phone number for a few minutes, trying to work out what 'TIME IS RUNNING OUT' means. The obvious being that we don't have long before we have another body on our hands, though I can't help but think that there is a deeper, hidden meaning.

'Maybe he means time is running out for you,' she says timidly, voicing the thought that had been running through my head all night. 'Maybe you should ask Bob for an officer to be stationed outside your house.'

I tell her I will consider it, though I know that I won't. I don't want to show a single strand of weakness, and I don't even know if the text message was a genuine threat towards me.

'We can't even be one hundred percent certain that Reuben is dead,' I say. 'The picture looks realistic but apparently he is known for these sorts of pranks. At least we know that the video was shot in a mill.'

I return to my office, taking a sip of the luke-warm coffee that has been left on my desk for a while and letting out a sigh.

The longer this case has rumbled on, the more frustrated I've become.

Rory and Ben, our two main suspects, are out there somewhere, probably laughing at our inability to catch them. No wonder the killer sent that text message. He was probably anticipating some high-octane game of cat and mouse and all he has been met with is a wall of silence. Perhaps that is what will drive him out into the open - his ego.

I open the internet browser and, against my better judgement, have a look at the news. Stories about *The Blood Ice Killer* dominate every website I click onto. I'd anticipated it, considering how many people had watched Reuben's last moments in the cinema, but I hadn't considered how far the news would spread. There are detailed accounts of his death on many websites. Some ballsier news outlets have even embedded a video of his swinging body on the cinema screen, captured on a mobile phone.

Actors, producers and, on one Fijian website, a soundman from *Blood Ice*, have used the opportunity in their favour. Little quotes about how sorry they are to hear of Reuben's passing nestle next to information about their next project. It makes me feel sick.

A ping from my computer signifies the arrival of an email. I unlock the computer and access my inbox. It appears Ross has worked his magic and has already converted the film. It arrives in the shape of an attached file, a pretty hefty one at that. I start the download and read the accompanying email text.

Hi Erika, please find attached the file of the film. Not a great watch, is it? Poor bastard. I did a bit of a rush job on the film because I thought you might need it ASAP, it's all there but the sound still isn't great. I'm still trying a few things to enhance the sound, so bear with me. It'll probably be tomorrow before you get my best efforts. Ross.

I have a strange feeling in my stomach. I don't really want to watch the film again. I know it's part of the job, but willingly watching a man have his life taken from him in a brutal manner requires a certain mindset. Still, it needs to be done. When the file is almost downloaded, I call out to Angela to assemble the team in the briefing room.

I GIVE THE TEAM a little insight into what it is they are about to watch, imploring them to look out for certain clues. Having seen the film once, I know the killing took place in one of the many mills dotted around the Greater Manchester area.

I pass this information onto the team and tell them that officers are looking for the body right now but, as there are hundreds of mills, the search could drag on. Hopefully, one of them will spot something to narrow down our hunt. Presumably the body has been left there for us to find and collect, all part of the killer's twisted game. I also refer to the snatch of speech that I couldn't quite make out first time around, the unknown man's voice that could be the biggest clue in the case yet. As everyone steels themselves, I press play.

The director's face fills the screen once more. There are a few intakes of breath at the level of violence and suffering his face shows. The room is silent as everyone's unbridled attention is fixed on the screen. Some are taking notes, scribbling in pads whilst keeping their eyes firmly glued on the action.

When the video reaches the point where the second man speaks, a few people sit up in their chairs and actively look like they are straining their ears for something; a hint of an accent or a regional expression. As Ross had warned me, the speech still sounds faint and garbled and there are no discernible words. I'm disappointed but I've got faith in Ross that he will be able to transform the words into something recognisable with a little more time.

The film rolls on and I watch again as Reuben's eyes widen and the crate is kicked from under him, his struggle against the tightened noose, his fingers searching for any hint of looseness but knowing there is none to be found. I watch the toes of his shoes almost make contact with the dusty, concrete floor and will him to extend his legs a fraction more. I sigh wistfully as his body becomes limp; the life draining out of him as the throes of death settle.

As the film ends, the room is filled with exhalations. It seems everyone had been holding their breath. Conversations erupt about what they have just seen and I let them discuss their points of view, before walking to the front of the room and trying to regain some sense of order. I hold my hand up and the noise mostly subsides.

'Did anyone notice anything of worth? I know the man who is off camera's speech is distorted, but what else have we got?' I ask the room.

Angela stands up and walks to the computer, moving the cursor of the film to the point where the crate gets kicked from under Reuben's feet. The frozen image stays on screen and she points to the boot.

'This looks like the same type of boot that would've left the marks on Anna's face and also in the mud at the end of the alley where Jay's body was found. I'd say the man behind the camera is the same man who has killed the others.'

She returns to her seat, amongst murmurs of agreement. Liam stands up, though he doesn't move from his place. He looks like he is struggling with what he is about to say, and I think I know why.

'Boss, that place,' he points at the screen that is still paused at the moment Reuben's fate was sealed.

The camera is at its most zoomed out and shows the cavernous room in all its glory; the uneven floor, the rickety stairs leading to a metal balcony and the faded sign of a company that used to call the warehouse its home before the recession forced job cuts. I didn't notice the sign on first viewing but now that I do, it's like an ice pick through my heart. The building where Reuben lost his life is the same building that I almost lost mine a year ago. The text message from the killer wasn't his only way of making this personal. Somehow, he knows what that place means to me. He chose it for a reason.

I walk to the phone, lift the receiver to my ear and punch in a number. A voice answers almost immediately.

'I know where the body is,' I say, my voice quivering, before reciting the address and setting down the phone. I turn back to the room. 'Let's catch this fucker.'

TOM IS SITTING AT one end of the sofa, flicking through Netflix, trying to find something for us to watch. My legs are draped over his, my feet pressed against the hard end of the sofa. I watch the brightly coloured graphics flick by, yet I don't take any of it in. My mind is elsewhere, though Tom hasn't seemed to notice. Or if he has, he's pretending that he hasn't.

Since he arrived just before dinner, he has been quiet, like he has something on his mind. He stops scrolling once he reaches some generic action film featuring a well-known action, flanked on the graphic by flames and an American muscle car. I've got no real desire to watch it, though I nod when he asks if I fancy it. At least I won't have to focus too hard to get a gist of the storyline.

I keep drifting back to the warehouse, and the untold violence that room has borne witness to. I picture the masked man creeping out of the shadows and lunging at me with the steel blade and the hate in his eyes. I shiver, trying to physically shake the memory away.

Tom throws the remote onto the carpeted floor as a fast-paced rock song and the squeal of car's tyres signal the start of the film. I quickly zone out, Reuben's body swinging from the noose filling my head, the boot kicking his link to life from under him; and I imagine the callous eyes of the unknown killer watching as soul leaves body. I want to scream at the lack of progress we have made and I am filled with envy that Tom can just switch off and get on with his day.

On the screen, the main character - a detective with a shaved head and a tight shirt which accentuates his bulging biceps - enters a house on a suburban street. In the living room, a badly mutilated body is found, a rouge teenager who had been missing for a while.

Tom laughs.

'Look at the crime scene. Have you ever seen one so organised and tidy? I'm afraid it's going to have to be a C- for the set designer.'

I laugh too. Everything in the room has been set purposefully by someone with an eye for detail. Shards of glass are littered artfully under the window and the television has been knocked over and the screen cracked in the middle. I've never seen a crime scene look so pretty.

Despite the unrealistic crime scene, I'm starting to enjoy the film when my phone emits a loud beep and I glance at the screen. An email from Ross has arrived. I immediately snatch up the phone and unlock it, navigating my way to the inbox to find an attached video file.

'It's about the case,' I reply, holding up my phone to show him the email I've just received. 'Do you mind if we watch it?'

'Of course,' he nods. 'This film is dreadful anyway.'

As I fetch my laptop from the kitchen and plump myself down onto the sofa beside Tom, his phone rings. He answers and walks out into the hallway. I can hear him attempting to calm someone before promising he will be leaving first thing in the morning and saying goodbye. He walks back in and I give him an inquisitive look.

'Dad,' he says, holding up the phone. 'Do you remember I mentioned I was going home for a few days to help dad look after mum? Well, he's nervous that I'd forgotten or couldn't do it anymore. He needs a break, poor man.'

'How is your mum?' I ask.

'She has her good days and bad days,' he answers, scratching his elbow. 'Alzheimer's is a bitch of a disease though. Anyway, I have to leave first thing in the morning – it's going to take me three hours or so to get Oxford.'

I give his leg and rub before logging into my emails and opening the newly received file from Ross.

The file is large for such a short film, which fills me with hope that the added data is the superior sound. Tom pours himself a beer and tops up my glass whilst the file downloads and with bated breath, I press play. For the third time, Reuben's battered face fills the screen. I watch as the action unfolds, noting sounds that I hadn't previously detected.

My heart begins to beat a little faster; the next few minutes could blow the whole case wide open. As the video nears the section in which the killer behind the camera speaks, I brace myself.

On screen, Reuben's speech is coming to an end. His bottom lip quivers and as he is about to continue, the other man speaks. Ross has done a phenomenal job with the audio as the speech is now as clear as day.

'Reuben, why did you kill my fiancée, Anna Symons?'

I've heard that question asked before, in the flesh and I now know who is on the other side of the camera. Tom and I exchange an excited look.

We have our killer.

Rory Knox.

25

'I APPRECIATE IT, BUT honestly, I'm fine,' says Ed, his dressing gown pulled tight to his body to shield him from the bitter evening wind.

As soon as I'd heard the voice on the recording with such clarity, I'd rang Ed to check on him. When there was no answer, I had raced around to Ed's house to make sure that he was OK.

The lights of the television emanating through the window as I made my way up the driveway had soothed my fears somewhat, and seeing him answer the door with a glass of scotch, unharmed, had alleviated them further. His phone had simply been charging in the kitchen.

However, his reluctance to leave his home and stay in a hotel for even a night, due to the fact that it is mere speculation that he may be next on Rory's list, is frustrating.

'At least let me station an officer outside,' I say.

Again, he shakes his head.

'I don't want to take up police resources. Look, if you are really this worried, I'll check in with you in the morning. And, if I feel even a little threatened during the night, I will take you up on the offer of some supervision outside the house.'

I can see that he is not going to budge, so I reluctantly agree to his plan. I remind him to be vigilant, bid him farewell and drive home.

When I return to my house, I am pleased to find I'd left the heating on, as it goes some way to warming my frozen hands. I gather the information we have on Rory and throw myself onto the sofa.

I spend some time poring over the case notes, hoping one little detail will jump out and change the case, though, after such a long day, I can feel my eyes growing heavy.

STAYING ALIVE BLASTS OUT from somewhere near my ear and I jerk awake, fully clothed on the sofa. I sit up straight, disorientated, and peer with barely open eyes at the time on the illuminated face of my digital watch. 3:07 am. I feel for the phone and squint at a number I don't recognise before pulling it to my ear.

'Hello,' I slur, wiping dribble from the side of my mouth.

'DI Piper, we've got him,' says a man's voice I can't quite place.

I implore my brain to wake up and attempt to conjure a face to go with the voice but I'm left grappling in the dark.

'DI Piper?' the man repeats into the silence.

'Sorry,' I reply, wiping the sleep from my eyes, 'you've got Rory?'

'We've got Ben McCall.'

I'm momentarily disappointed that it's not Rory who has been apprehended, but I suppose I did only call it in a few hours previously. Ben is still a coup.

I push the case notes on to the floor and push myself upright, telling the man on the other end of the phone that I'm on my way to meet them at the station.

'I'd hold fire,' he answers, 'the lad is absolutely smashed, can barely string a sentence together. He'll be right as rain after a few hours in a cell. Get a bit more sleep and he'll be waiting for you in the morning.'

'Thank you. Good job,' I say and hang up, remembering his name is Craig just a second too late.

I turn off the lights in the living room and make my way into the bedroom, pulling on a pair of pyjamas and jumping into bed.

I turn the pillow onto the cold side and plant my head into it. The bed feels enormous without Tom, who had accompanied me to Ed's house but left for his own home afterwards, on account of his early start.

Now that I'm awake and alone, I can't stop thinking about the video and the fact we now have our killer but no clue where he is or how to find him.

By the time I check my phone again, I realise that I've been lying in my bed, awake, for over an hour. *What a waste of time* I think to myself as I drag my body out of bed and set about locating my long-forgotten, or rather long-ignored, running gear.

Eventually, I find a pile of shorts and t-shirts unceremoniously dumped in the bottom of my wardrobe. I whisper my apologies to them and pull them on; judging them to be a little tighter since I last wore them. I slip on my trainers, which still have a timing chip from a local 10k intertwined between the laces, and head for the door.

Ten minutes later, I'm fighting against my scorching lungs which are protesting at the unheralded burst of physical activity. For a December morning, it's surprisingly mild. The air is cold as it enters my lungs, trying to sate the burning, though there is a comfort in it.

I refuse to yield to the pain and pick up the pace, the motivational messages from issues of running magazines on a loop in my head. I run down Dan Bank and stop at the traffic lights before turning round and ascending the steep hill, stopping at the top momentarily to catch my breath, before taking off again.

All the while, the case circles my head, every synapse firing, trying to find a little avenue we haven't yet explored. We now know that Rory Knox murdered Reuben Amaro. This is a fact, we have it on video. And we have a motive; he believes that Reuben murdered his fiancé and this is simply payback.

However, based on the CCTV footage from outside Limas and the hotel, it appears that Reuben did nothing more than try to help Anna in any way he could.

This means that Rory probably took his revenge on the wrong person, and that Anna's killer is still at large, meaning we are no closer to catching him now, than on the night the body was discovered on the ice.

This means there are two killers on the loose, unless, of course, Rory also killed Anna and only killed the others in an attempt to cover his tracks.

I turn into my street and sprint as fast as I can to my door, bending over with my hands on my knees, gulping in the morning air trying not to be sick all over my driveway.

Once I know that I'm not going to throw up, I remove the key from the zipped pocket on the back of my leggings and let myself into my house, heading up the stairs and straight to the bathroom. It takes a while to clamber out of my tight, sweaty clothes and when I do, I climb into the shower.

As the water pours over me, my mind turns to Ben. He is in custody right now, probably still attempting to sleep off a night on the tiles. I imagine his lanky frame contorted, trying to get comfortable on the poor excuse for a bed in the holding cell. I imagine his fear as his actions over the past few weeks may about to be laid bare.

THE SURPRISE MUST BE etched all over my face at the sight of DCI Bob standing by my desk. It is 8:30 a.m. and I have arrived at work a little early to prepare for Ben's interview. I hadn't expected him back for another week at least, so to see him standing here is a shock.

'The wife is sick of me,' he says as I approach, answering the question before I've asked it. 'She needs to rest and doesn't appreciate being asked if she wants anything every few minutes. She begged me to come back to work, especially in light of the evidence gathered from the video. Good work, Erika.'

I feel a rush of pride at the compliment, as DCI Bob is a notoriously hard man to please. However, I'm quickly brought back down to earth by his next statement.

'I am going to lead the interview with,' he pauses and checks the notes he is holding in his hand, 'Ben McCall.'

He doesn't offer any further information, and I don't ask, though I do feel indignant.

I'm the one who has a relationship with Ben, having met him at the bookstore. I'm the one who brought him to the attention of my superior and I am the one who has done the legwork, literally, in trying to apprehend him.

'We're going to bring him out soon, we're just waiting for his lawyer to arrive,' he adds, before excusing himself and sauntering off in the direction of the toilets.

I'VE TAKEN MY PLACE in the observation room, behind the one-way glass. My breath forms a mist on the cold surface, making me realise that I'm too close to the glass. I'm just dying to be in there, instead of being sat on the subs bench.

Ben looks like he is nursing a particularly painful hangover. His eyes are sunken and bloodshot, and his forehead is coated in a film of sweat. He keeps reaching for the bottle of water in front of him and then thinking better of it, his fingers going back to drumming a rhythm on the table instead.

His thick hair is wilder than ever, jutting out in all directions. He's wearing a brightly patterned, short sleeve shirt and a pair of skinny jeans; clothes carefully chosen for a night out by the looks of things.

DCI Bob finishes the introductions for the recording device's benefit and moves on to the questions. Ben sneaks a nervous glance at his lawyer, who is the polar opposite of the student in every way. His faded grey suit is ill fitting and the buttons on his well-worn shirt are stretched to their limit by his huge gut. His hair is thinning, his face ruddy and his jowls wobble as he shakes his head at something. He doesn't look like the type of man you'd entrust your fate to, though looks can be deceiving.

I've watched Mr Gareth Price in action before; the man is formidable. For each of DCI Bob's opening questions, the lawyer interrupts before Ben has a chance to even open his mouth.

'My client won't be answering that question at this stage,' he says, again and again and I can sense DCI Bob's frustration growing.

'Look,' says Ben, peering at the lawyer like a naughty schoolchild, 'all I want to do is clear this up. The reason I ran away from the police that day is because I'd been smoking weed. I saw the police car and freaked, OK?'

The lawyer is doing well to contain his annoyance, though I can see a muscle in his jaw tighten.

'I wasn't thinking and I know how it looks, but I can hand-on-heart say that I haven't murdered anyone.'

DCI Bob's countenance brightens immediately. There's almost the hint of a smile. 'Tell me about what happened outside the pub on the night of the fifth of December, the night Jason Krist was murdered.'

Ben looks at his lawyer, who gives an almost imperceptible nod, so he launches into a story about how he had followed Jay to the pub in order to apologise and ask for advice on how to make it as a film maker but chickened out.

As he is explaining why he took refuge in the alley, the door of the observation room opens, allowing a shaft of light to enter the darkened room. Angela beckons me with a curled finger and I turn away from the one-way glass, following her to her desk.

'Sorry about tearing you away from the interview, Erika, it's just, I've got... news,' she says.

She sits down on her chair and spins it so that she is face to face with her computer screen. Clicking a few icons, she brings up a map which shows an aerial view of Manchester city centre and the surrounding towns. There are a dozen or so small red dots in total, almost in a triangular formation. I kneel down to get a better view.

'What exactly am I looking at here?' I ask her.

'It seems Mr Rory Knox is back in the North,' she answers. 'The red spots are the locations Rory's car has triggered an ANPR camera. Mostly in the city centre, but a few down towards Altrincham, presumably visiting Anna's mother again.'

I pull over another chair and sit down, studying the map. Why has he suddenly made a re-appearance? He must know that his little video has made a splash and been brought to the attention of the police.

Maybe he's back to find his next victim. It's more important, now than ever, that we find Rory Knox. I tell Angela to keep me in the loop and that the next time his car is recognised, to let me know straight away.

Angela produces a print out of the map and I take it to my room, setting it on top of the paper work I've been neglecting.

I phone Ed again. He answers quickly and tells me that he has had an uninterrupted night's sleep and that there is no sign of anything happening out of his front window. I tell him I will be in touch later to make sure he is still OK, and he laughs, which makes me feel like his over-protective mother.

I set the phone down, feeling slightly annoyed that Ed isn't taking his own care more seriously, and as I get up to return to the observation booth, I see Ben and the lawyer walking towards the door, apparently done with the interview.

Ben casts a glance my way and gives a slight nod of his head coupled with a thin, closed-mouthed smile. Maybe it's an apology for running away or maybe it's a covert celebration from a man who is currently getting away with murder.

Ben and his lawyer walk side-by-side into the lift and the door closes, obscuring them from view. I run to the stairs, taking two at a time, and arrive on the ground floor as the lift doors re-open and the two men walk out.

I hide behind a wall as they sign out at the reception desk, before leaving the building together. I creep to the window and watch a relieved-looking Ben shake hands with his lawyer.

Gareth opens the door to a sleek Mercedes estate, throws his briefcase onto the passenger seat and takes his place behind the wheel. He says something to Ben who shakes his head and points up the street, before closing the door and speeding out of the car park.

Ben, now alone, leans against a lamppost and fishes a packet of cigarettes from his jacket pocket. As he closes the lid of his lighter and puffs out a plume of smoke, I make my way out onto the street and approach him.

'What do *you* want?' he asks, the confidence he displayed on the night I first encountered him back on show.

'Five minutes of your time.'

'I've already told your boss everything I know,' he replies.

'I'll buy you a pint,' I say, pointing at the pub across the road.

BEN GULPS DOWN ALMOST a third of his pint and when he sets it down on the table, froth has settled into his patchy beard. He wipes it away with the back of his hand and fixes his intense eyes on mine.

'What do you want to know then?' he asks, his chest puffed out.

'What happened in the alleyway?'

For the first time, I see a little of his coolness ebb away, allowing fear to creep in. His walls come down and he tells me every detail of what happened, and I believe every word he says.

He tells me that he went into the alley on a whim, to try and build up the courage to approach Jay. He acknowledges that it was a long time to be in the alley, that he was looking at his phone and simply lost track of time, but when he heard another person enter the alley, he was frightened, so he hid behind one of the cars.

He then heard the other man calling out. He was scared. He was about to make a break for it, when Jay walked into the alley towards the sound, so stayed put. He listened as Jay's footsteps became fainter as he walked past the car park and further towards the bottom of the sloping alleyway.

Tears spring into his eyes as he recalls the noise of whatever it was smashing into Jay's body, the sound of bones breaking and a life ending. He says he almost vomited behind the car as the killer made his way past him onto the street, but just managed to hold it in.

He tells me that the night will haunt him forever, and that the thought of making a film with even one death is too much for him and that he is considering changing courses, or leaving university altogether.

I sit back in my chair and when I look at Ben now, I see him in a completely different light. He was simply in the wrong place at the wrong time, and bore witness to something life changing. I see a lost young man who will never be the same again. And I actually feel sorry for him.

I thank him for his time, and offer him a lift back to his halls which he declines. I leave him sitting at the table, nursing his almost empty pint glass.

Outside, I send Tom a text message asking if he got to Oxford safely. As I make my way back to the police station for DCI Bob's debrief, Tom replies with a simple 'yes.' I'm surprised at the brevity of the message, though I can't imagine how difficult it must be for him, watching his mum's slow decline. I type 'see you soon' and hit send, before entering the doors of the station.

AMY SITS OPPOSITE ME once more. I'd almost forgotten about the therapy appointment, on account of how hectic my day had been. Luckily, Amy had called to change the time and so I hadn't missed it.

'Welcome back,' she says.

We exchange small talk about our week before she takes on a more professional expression.

'I know last week we flitted around a lot and had a really good discussion about lots of things, but this week I'd really like to know more about the night in the mill.'

My heart sinks at the thought of once again dredging up the memory of almost dying, but I suppose that this is exactly what these sessions are for. I sigh and ask her what she wants to know.

'Everything.'

My mind drifts back to the night in question and I begin to tell Amy my tale, leaving no detail unsaid.

The abandoned mill looked even more imposing in the darkness. We had received intel that day that suggested one of the most wanted men in the area was using the mill as a place to hide. Liam and I had been tasked with staking it out that night, though Liam was running late and had arranged to meet me as soon as he could.

I had rejected the offer of another partner; after all, all I had to do was sit in the car and keep watch. A short while later, I saw the silhouetted body of, what I presumed was our target, glancing around the area before disappearing inside. I radioed it in and DCI Bob told me to keep watching.

Not long after that, I heard a scream from inside the mill. My mind raced with possibilities. Aside from the person I'd seen enter, no one else had gone in. I thought that maybe he had a hostage in there, or that perhaps someone just as dangerous had been waiting on him returning.

Either way, with a life in danger, you act.

'So, I phoned DCI Bob and told him about the scream. He told me to get in there. I asked him if I should wait on back-up and he said no.'

I look at Amy, tears threatening to spill.

'Is that an order? I asked and he replied 'Yes.' So I ran into the building, expecting to see some sort of violent scene, though all I was greeted with was darkness. Then, I heard a shuffling and a man, dressed from head to toe in black, crawled out from under some pipework. He looked murderous.'

I breathe.

'I assumed in that moment that he had seen the police car and had screamed to try and lure me in. Then he lunged at me with the blade and it becomes a bit of a blur after that.'

Amy has remained composed during my tale, scribbling notes covertly and nodding in all the right places. She sets down her notepad and looks me straight in the eye.

'Do you blame Bob?' she asks.

The tears flow in earnest now, and, unable to speak, I simply nod my head. I hadn't thought of it that way before.

I SINK INTO THE sofa and take a sip from my glass. I considered cracking open a bottle of wine, but I need a clear head to make sense of the case, so I've opted for an ice-cold lemonade. It feels like we're closing in.

We know Rory is back in the city, which means that another murder could be about to happen. Obviously, we can't let that happen, so it is imperative that we keep a close eye on his whereabouts through the network of ANPR cameras. It seems possible that he doesn't know that is a method of surveillance.

It's also possible that there is another killer too. It seems that Reuben's murder was in retaliation to Anna's, with Rory apparently thinking that Reuben was her killer and doling out what he saw as an appropriate punishment.

It could also be the case that Rory is the only killer, and that his part in the video was an act to detract attention from himself. We know that Jay threw Rory off set, which may or may not have played a part in Reuben and Anna getting together.

If Rory had remained on set, the actor and director would never have had the opportunity to get close. Perhaps Rory holds Jay responsible for the tumultuous period in their relationship.

DCI Bob has accepted that Ben is not culpable, as he has an alibi for his whereabouts during the time of Anna's death. Which leaves Ed as the only other possibility. There is motive there for at least one of the murders; his fractious relationship with Jay is well documented, though why would he kill Anna? He spoke warmly about her and the brief time they spent together on set. He also has no reason to kill his best friend. All signs point to Rory.

I pick up the map for the hundredth time today and survey the dots, peppered around the city like little redcurrants. I try again to find some sort of pattern, some rhyme or reason to his travels.

I use the maps application on my phone to look at the most heavily populated areas of the dots. One of the group of dots is near the ice rink where Anna was murdered, which is also close to Anna's mother's house.

It is well documented that serial killers are often drawn back to the scene of their own crimes. Is Rory using his time in the city to visit the place he enacted his ultimate revenge on his cheating fiancée?

The two other groups of dots are in the city centre, the app calculating their distance to be eleven minutes by car.

I make a note of the areas and decide to visit them in the morning.

26

'DO YOU RECOGNISE THIS MAN?' I ask the receptionist. Her name badge informs us she is called Helen. Her grey hair is short and has been cut with a straight fringe. Large golden hooped earrings rest on her hunched shoulders and wrinkles at the corners of her eyes suggest she may be approaching retirement. She is sat behind a counter in the foyer of a chain hotel. I have just passed her a picture of Rory and she studies it for a minute before nodding her head.

'Yes,' she confirms. 'He stayed here for a number of nights, though he checked out early this morning.'

'Did you notice anything unusual about him?' Liam asks.

She shakes her head. She taps a few keys and studies the screen, before shaking her head again. She tells us that he has no notes on his room – no damage, no outstanding bills, nothing of note.

Someone tuts from behind us and I turn to see an agitated man with carefully coiffed hair and round, turtle shell glasses. He is grasping a bright yellow holdall on wheels. Once he sees that we are police and not guests of the hotel who are taking an extraordinary time to check out, he attempts to turn the tutting into a little, relaxed rhythm - without success. He looks away under the weight of my stare.

With nothing else to learn about Rory's stay in the hotel, we thank the receptionist and make our way to the door, which slides open upon our approach. With confirmation that Rory stayed here, two thirds of the ANPR dots are accounted for. Now, it's time to verify the final third.

A QUARTER OF AN hour later, we pull up in front of a row of run-down shops and Liam looks slightly anxious about leaving the car in such an area. I grab the picture of Rory from the back seat and walk into the shop on the end of the row.

The newsagents is full to bursting with discounted stock. Brightly coloured card, cut into the shapes of firework explosions, display appealing prices and buy-one-get-one-free offers. Boxes full of multipack, not for individual resale crisps line one wall and a bored-looking man with his hair brushed forward and a mono-brow, who is on his phone and speaking rapidly in a language I do not understand, sits behind a shelf full of assorted chocolate bars.

'Do you recognise this man?' I ask, holding the photograph of Rory above the display of food. He doesn't stop his phone call and barely looks at the picture before waving his hand and shaking his head. We leave the shop without another word, whilst he continues his conversation.

'The big man needs to work on his customer service,' Liam remarks, as we make our way into the next shop. The same uncooperative attitude follows us down the row, until we get to a doorway with a metallic shutter pulled over it. The sign above the doorway shows that the premises are used as a massage parlour and through an eye-level slot, presumably used as a letter box, I can see a set of stairs. I ring the bell and a lady's voice crackles through the intercom system.

'Not open 'til five, sorry.'

I press the button at the bottom of the communication device, hopefully allowing whoever is upstairs to hear me. I explain who we are, why we are here and ask her to come to the door. A minute later, a pair of eyes are looking at us through the slot.

I hold the picture of Rory up so that whoever is behind the door has an unhindered view, and the look in her eyes tells me we have found someone who knows Rory.

'Harry,' says the woman, in a thick Eastern European accent. Liam and I look at each other.

'May we come in?' I ask. The woman nods and makes her way back up the stairs. I am about to ring the bell again, assuming she has misunderstood me, when the shutters begin to rise off the ground. It stops halfway up, forcing Liam and I both to bend down and shimmy underneath it. As we make our way up the stairs, the mechanical noise of the shutter starts again and I turn to watch it clash with the pavement, sealing us in.

At the top of the stairs is a small room, with a corridor branching off containing four identical doors. The walls have been painted a brilliant white and reflect the fluorescent pink strip lights. A makeshift desk serves as a reception area and laminated posters on the wall advertise the services available here, as well as the prices.

'Is anyone else here?' I ask.

The woman shakes her head. She has closely cropped dark hair and is wearing a short satin dressing gown, which exposes thin legs. She opens a door and leads us into a room with a table and chairs, a clothes stand with an array of outfits and an open chest containing a mixture of wigs, in all styles and colours. I figure that this is the reason why her hair has been cut so short – to allow her to become whoever a customer wants her to be. We sit down on a chair and I put the photograph on the table.

'So you know this man?' Liam says.

She nods. Liam rotates his hand, trying to elicit a more comprehensive answer.

'Harry. Came here a lot of nights.'

I struggle to place the accent.

'For a massage?' Liam ventures.

'First night, sex. He try but he can't. Too sad. He say bad thing happen to him and he do bad thing too. He not want massage. He still pay.'

'You said on the first night, he paid you to have sex with him, but he couldn't do it. Did he come back again?' I ask.

She nods her head.

'For sex?'

'No,' she shakes her head. 'For friends. He nice man. He say he do bad thing but I don't think yes. Wife died. He wants friends. Spend a lot of time here.'

'Do you think he will be here tonight?' I enquire.

'No,' she says, sadly. 'My boyfriend. Suspicious. He come last night. Harry too. He think Harry more than customer. My boyfriend angry. He threaten Harry with knife. Harry run.'

Liam and I look at each other. So Rory spent a number of evenings here, under a different identity, and seemingly paid for her time to just sit with him. Now he's been scared off with a knife, I wonder where he will go next.

'This man, I say, pointing at the picture, 'is called Rory, not Harry. We think he might be dangerous. Did he ever try to hurt you?'

She shakes her head.

'Did he say what the bad thing was?' Liam asks.

She repeats the action with her head.

I give her one of my cards, explaining to her that if he does come back here, she should phone me straight away. She nods and I think she understands the severity of the situation. We leave the room and walk to the desk where she presses a button, and in the distance, I can hear the shutters moving. Before we leave, she gives us a leaflet with information about the business. A photograph of her with the name Luna underneath is included on the back, next to a selection of other women. We bid her goodbye and leave the parlour with some answers and more questions.

THE ALMOST IMPOSSIBLE QUIZ show is infuriating, yet I can't stop watching, though I haven't got a question correct yet. I am about to go to the toilet when my phone begins to ring.

'Angela?'

'Boss!' she sounds breathless. 'Rory is on the move, his car triggered one of the cameras in the west of the city about ten minutes ago. I've already got in touch with officers in the vicinity and they are keeping an eye out. I'll let you know if we get him.'

She hangs up before I have a chance to reply. My stomach tightens at the thought of Rory's capture. The net is closing in. Time for a celebratory drink. I push myself off the sofa and head to the kitchen, picking a chilled bottle of white wine from the fridge. As I pop the cork, I hear my phone vibrate against the wooden table.

I leave the open wine bottle and race into the living room, snatching the phone to my ear without looking at the screen.

'Have we got him?' I say, a little louder than I meant to.

There is no reply from the other end of the phone, though I can hear heavy breathing. I pull the phone away from my ear and am surprised when I realise it is a call from an unknown number. I thought it was Angela with good news.

'Hello?' I say into the phone, elongating the word like I'm in a film.

'DI Piper?' whispers a voice. I assure them that it is who they think it is a wait for them to speak again.

'It's Ed,' he says, still in a whisper, 'I think there is someone in my house.'

My mind springs straight to Rory. His car has been spotted in the region of the city where Ed's house is, and if Rory is set on continuing his killing spree, it seems probable that Ed would be next on his list, having been involved, however tenuously in the creation of *Blood Ice*.

Rory might even believe that Ed is the most blameworthy, having created the universe that the film took place in. Without

Ed's *Threat* trilogy, there might never have been any of these murders.

'Okay, tell me what's happening,' I reply.

There's another minute of silence before he whispers his answer. 'I heard a huge crash from downstairs, sounded like the door was being kicked in.'

'And where are you now?'

'Upstairs. I'm in the...' he trails off.

I wait for him to talk again, not wanting to disturb him. When he speaks again, it's almost inaudible. 'I think he's coming upstairs.'

There's a shuffling noise and I assume that Ed is attempting to conceal himself as best he can. This is followed by loud thuds, which sound like heavy footsteps.

'YOU!' shouts Ed, all of a sudden, making me jump.

There appears to be a struggle on the other end of the phone before he can finish his sentence. There's some grunting and shouting as the fight continues and a few seconds later, the line goes dead.

27

'I'VE JUST TURNED INTO his street,' I shout into the radio.

The rain is coming down in torrents and visibility is low. I slow the car to manoeuvre around vehicles parked on kerbs outside houses, though their bulk partially blocks the road.

Once outside Ed's house, I pull up on the kerb and kill the engine. I stare into the darkness of the house, wondering if another body awaits me. I keep the engine running so that the car continues to be filled with heat.

The static hiss of the radio makes me jump, before Liam's voice sounds, informing me that he is not far behind and warning me in no uncertain terms to wait for him before entering the house.

I assure him that I will wait, and pull out a pair of blue, protective gloves from a box in the glove compartment and slip them on. Liam shows up a few minutes later and parks just in front, hitting the kerb a little faster than intended.

He jumps out of his car and gives me a little nod, pulling the hood of his coat over his head. I turn my keys and pull them out of the ignition, before pocketing them and joining Liam outside. The clock on my phone tells me that it has just gone past quarter to eight, though the oppressive rainclouds and deserted street make it feel more like the middle of the night.

I bemoan the heavy rain that is still pouring from the heavens; worrying about the evidence it could interfere with, though Liam assures me that the forensic team aren't far behind him.

As we walk up the path, I see the front door has been forcibly removed from its hinges. It is lying on its side, half inside and half outside. I get my phone from my pocket and select the torch icon, letting the light flood the area.

Some of the plastic on the PVC door frame has been snapped away and a small amount of blood is present. I bend down to take a closer look and deduce that Ed has probably been taken from his home by whoever broke in. Ed must've put up one final attempt at freedom on the doorstep, wrapping his fingers round the door frame and clinging on with all his might.

This is a welcome find for two reasons; it means we are probably not going to find Ed's lifeless body within the walls of the house and it could mean we have a chance of locating him before he meets his maker.

We move through the hall and into the living room, which has been trashed. The sofa stands untouched amongst the debris, a lone survivor amongst the chaos. The drinks cabinet-cum-table has been tipped on its side, causing the bottles of assorted alcohols to tip and smash, showering the room in broken glass and making it smell like a particularly grotty pub at last orders. The television has been pushed to the ground and the curtain pole ripped from its fittings above the bay window.

Careful not to touch anything, as I don't want to risk suffering the wrath of Martin and the forensics team, we make our way upstairs to confirm there is no body present. We open the doors and peek into a few rooms, though only the bathroom and Ed's bedroom have suffered the same fate as the living room, the rest remain untouched.

Happy that there is no body, we make our way back down the stairs and wait outside for the forensic team.

MARTIN IS DOING WELL not to show his annoyance. He smiled cheerily as he stepped out of his van and remained almost impassive as we told him we had been in the house to confirm the lack of a corpse.

Even though he knows, as detectives, we are fully entitled to do so, Martin is of the impression that forensics should always be the first to have access to a crime scene, for fear of losing a modicum of evidence.

His team work quickly to secure the area and before long, a perimeter has been established. The flashing blue lights of the patrol cars have piqued the neighbours' interest. Silhouetted bodies are evident in a number of neighbouring windows, peering out into the cold night, whilst some have pulled coats on and are braving the rain, huddling close to the tape separating the street from the crime scene, trying to ascertain some information from the stationed officers, who remain impassive.

An hour or so later, Martin grants us access to the house. His team are still working, but as there is no body, he sees no harm with us being in there at the same time, providing we stick to his strict protocol - no touching shit without his consent; his words.

Careful not to move any of the little yellow numbered markers indicating something of interest, we make our way through the downstairs area of the house. Having already looked in the living room, and trusting Martin's judgement that there isn't much more to be gleaned from the room, we make our way into the kitchen.

It puts my little kitchen to shame. A double range-style cooker is fitted between bespoke, heavy wooden cabinets with stainless steel handles. A large marble island sits pride of place in the middle of the floor, housing a block of knives and a set of wooden cutting boards. An oversized American style fridge freezer fills the back wall and a door to the right of it leads to a vast expanse of a dining room.

It seems no expense has been spared in decorating and furnishing. It also seems a little grandiose for a single man, but I suppose if you have the money, you may as well spend it. You can't take it with you.

Martin appears at the door and informs Liam and me that nothing of evidential interest has been found in this area of the house. Liam turns to leave and I follow suit, before stopping when I notice a card on the kitchen island, partially wrapped in its envelope.

Checking that Martin isn't watching me, I slip the card out of its holdings and take a peek inside. It is addressed to Ed's mum and underneath the generic, mass printed happy birthday message, Ed has signed his name.

The calligraphy is familiar, though I can't place it. It looks like it has been scrawled quickly and is written in capitals. I snap a photograph of it on my phone, and then leave the kitchen and catch up with Liam, who has one foot on the first stair.

The door squeaks as I push it open, revealing Ed's bedroom. It's as it was before, though now I notice some blood on the duvet cover; perhaps this is where he was hiding when he was found.

We have a poke around, but there is not much else to be found in here. I note that the mannequin head is no longer lying on the floor, but standing upright on the bedside cabinet. The face has had a makeover and no longer appears angry. The eyebrows are angled and the lip-sticked mouth now resembles a shocked face.

Fully aware that the crime scene photographer will have taken pictures of every room from every conceivable angle, I still slip out my phone and take a few photos for my own edification. With one last glance, I pull the door closed again and join Liam in the bathroom.

There are drops of blood on the floor and the smear of a bloody handprint on the side of the bath. I can't help but think of *Psycho*, especially with the way the shower curtain is hanging. The cabinet above the sink diverts my attention from the bath. The mirrored cabinet has been unlocked; the small, metal lock sits on the sink in a small pool of residual water. The door is ajar and, flying in the face of Martin's rule, I pull it open, expecting to find bags of white powder or worse.

However, there are no illegal substances to be found. A few over-the-counter tablet packets lie on their sides. One open packet in particular catches my eye, as it has a sticker across the front. It doesn't have a name, but it does have this address and the prescriptive instructions for the medication.

I take my phone out and snap a picture of the box, focussing on the name of the tablets, Promethazine (Phenergan). The instructions are thorough and I realise from the label that they must be professionally prescribed and very powerful.

I remember my mum saying that the more names a medicine has, the worse the illness must be. I slip my phone back into my pocket and leave the bathroom, closing the door behind me.

As I close the door, I can feel my phone vibrate. Angela's name flashes on the screen and as I put the phone to my ear, it slips from my hand and drops to the floor.

Luckily, the thick carpet absorbs the impact and when I pick it up, it is still ringing. Ignoring the annoyed look from one of the forensic technicians, I carefully accept the call and press it to my ear.

'Boss?'

'Yes, how's it going Angela? Any more information on Rory and his whereabouts?'

'We do. His car triggered another ANPR hit and it looks like he is heading towards the motorway exit used to access Anna's mothers address in Altrincham.'

Even though Anna's mum is convinced of Rory's innocence, my blood runs cold at the thought of him on the loose, potentially having dumped Ed's body somewhere, dead or alive. Maybe he's planning on killing everyone he can who is connected with his ex-fiancée.

When I try to reply, I find my mouth has gone dry and no sound comes out.

'Boss?' Angela repeats.

'I'm on my way,' I manage to get out.

THE ROADS ARE QUIET and it doesn't take long to navigate our way to Altrincham. The driveway is empty as we make our way past the house. We turn a corner and park the car a little farther up the road, careful to remain as inconspicuous as possible; a hard task in a police car with luminous stripes along the side.

'Did you ring ahead?' asks Liam as he gets out of the car.

I slam my door closed.

'No,' I reply. 'I thought about it but I didn't want to give Rory a head start if he's already there.'

There are no lights on in the house, despite it only being shortly after ten o'clock. Anna's mother must be a fan of an early night. I push the gate and hold it open for Liam, who walks through with a nod of his head before knocking firmly on the door. I make sure the gate has latched properly before going to stand at his side.

For a while, there is no movement. Then, a light illuminates the frosted pane of glass to the side of the door.

'Who is it?' says a cracked voice.

'DI Piper and DS Sutton,' I respond, pushing my ID against the glass window. The scrape of the latch sounds and the door opens slowly, revealing Anna's mother. She is wearing flowery pyjamas, her hair is messy and her eyes haven't opened fully yet.

'Come in,' she utters, 'you'll catch your death out there.'

We follow her once more into the living room and take a seat. 'You'll have to excuse my attire, I can't stand the darkness of the winter nights so I take myself off to bed. Usually with a book, but tonight I must've drifted off straight away,' she says when she has sat down opposite us.

'We're sorry that we are here at this time, but we have a few important questions that couldn't wait,' I say, trying to keep my voice level so as not to worry her, though I can see that she looks apprehensive.

'Have you seen Rory since we last spoke?'

She shakes her head.

'Any contact at all?'

'None,' she answers, shaking her head again. 'Why?'

I consider my answer. I do not want to worry her unnecessarily, but it is important she realises that he is a dangerous man.

'We have reason to believe that he is back in the area, and we think that he is dangerous.'

I decide against telling her that he most probably murdered her daughter.

She looks sceptical.

'He isn't. He has been here lots of times since Anna was… you know… I really don't think he's capable of what you're saying.'

Her eyes fill with tears and I know she must be thinking of her only child. I push the box of tissues that are sitting on the table towards her.

'Either way,' I begin, once she has dabbed at her eyes, 'do you have somewhere else you could sleep tonight? A relative's house, perhaps, or with a friend?'

In the space of time between my question and her answer, there is the faint sound of metal scraping against metal, coming from outside the door. Then, the unmistakable sound of the gate being closed. A moment later, there is a loud, urgent knock on the door.

I instinctively reach for my gun, my hand wrapping around the handle. Liam does the same. I whisper to Anna's mother to go upstairs to the bathroom and to lock the door. She gives us a terrified look before following our orders, as another powerful knock on the door interrupts the silence in the house.

Liam walks towards the door, gun at his side. He unlocks the door and presses down on the handle, before taking a quick step back and extending his arms in front of him, gun raised.

Standing in the doorway is Rory. There is a deep gash on his arm and he is holding a toolbox in his left hand.

28

'SO WHAT HAPPENED AFTER you arrested him?'

DCI Bob, Liam and I are sat in his office. It's nearly midnight and I can feel the exhaustion of the frenetic day settling into my body. I rub my eyes in an attempt to clear some of the fog, and describe what happened after Liam opened the door. How Rory had dropped the hammer and claimed it wasn't what it looked like and how he hadn't resisted when we asked him to accompany us to the police station for questioning. In fact, he had come very willingly. Of course, he had no choice.

Bob looks annoyed.

'I don't know what fucking game he is playing, but it's time to find out,' he spits, standing up and moving around his desk.

He motions for me to follow him into the interview room, currently being occupied by Rory.

Looking through the window, he appears agitated. He's sitting at a right angle to the table, one fidgeting leg draped across the other. His elbow is resting on the flat surface, his hand palm down, with fingers drumming rhythmically on the table. When the door opens, he slowly swivels his head and greets us with a worried smile.

'I think I'd like my lawyer now,' he says before Bob or I can say a word.

'Perfect,' utters Bob, before marching out of the room. I tell Rory that his lawyer will be contacted, though it will be morning before the interview will take place and that a cell will be made up for him to stay the night. His face falls at this information and I leave without another word.

I GLANCE AT MY watch as DCI Bob launches into the introductory spiel. It's 9:03AM. Rory is sitting opposite me, looking even less composed than last night. His shirt is wrinkled and he looks sweaty, his hair greasy. The darkness under his eyes suggests he hasn't had a very restful night.

The man sitting next to him, on the other hand, looks ready to go, despite presumably being up most of the night preparing for today. His angular jawline is covered in designer stubble and his dark hair is flecked with grey. His suit looks expensive and the pressed white shirt paired with a light pink tie lend him a sophisticated air.

He introduces himself as James Poole and I'm slightly taken aback by the London accent. Less The Only Way is Essex, more Made in Chelsea.

'That's a pretty nasty gash,' DCI Bob says, pointing at Rory's now bandaged forearm.

'It's nothing,' replies Rory, dropping his arm to his side and out of view.

'If you insist,' DCI Bob says. 'Right, let's get started. Why…'

'Rory, we know about what happened with Luna at the massage parlour,' I interject.

His eyes widen and he glances at his lawyer, who looks as if he has been blindsided. DCI Bob looks furiously at me for interrupting him.

'That's how I got this cut,' he says, holding up his bandaged arm.

'Why did you visit there?' I ask.

He breathes a deep sigh. 'After Anna died…'

'You mean, after you murdered Anna,' DCI Bob states, trying to rile him.

Rory doesn't rise to the bait.

'After Anna died,' he tries again, looking in turn from his lawyer to me, 'I went to her mother's house. She was alone and so was I. I thought it would be helpful for both of us. But it was too intense. We talked about Anna and when we didn't talk about her, we were thinking about her. It was too much. So, I upped one day and left, with the intention of coming back to finish those jobs. I checked into a cheap hotel and stayed in the city centre. I drank a lot. Every morning, once I was sober enough, I'd drive towards her house, but I couldn't do it. I had to pass the ice rink to get there, and every time, it freaked me out.'

He wipes his nose on the bandage. His eyes drop to the floor as he continues his story.

'I ended up at some massage place I found online. The first night, I paid some poor girl for sex, but when it came to it, I couldn't follow through. She was kind and listened to me. It turns out I didn't want sex, all I wanted was someone to talk to. Someone who hadn't known Anna.'

'She said you were talking about a bad thing,' I state.

He hesitates. 'When I was in Bradford, I saw a picture of Anna and Reuben together, in that bar. I was furious. I couldn't believe that she had lied to me when she told me she was having an early night. It hurt. So, I got drunk and slept with some girl I met in the first bar I went to.'

He looks like he wishes the floor would open up.

'That's the bad thing,' he whispers. 'While my fiancée was being murdered, I was shagging some stranger.'

I think back to our first interview with Rory.

'When we showed you the CCTV footage of Anna leaving the bar with Reuben and Ed, it seemed like you hadn't known they were together.'

He scratches the back of his head.

'I know,' he says, almost apologetically. 'I knew they were together in the bar, but I didn't know they had left together. I was genuinely angry when I saw the footage.'

His eyes look a little wet and he takes a few calming breaths. While he composes himself, I set the good luck card we recovered from Anna's bedroom in front of him.

'Did you send this?' I ask, opening to show the words inside – *One day, you'll get what you deserve.*

He nods his head in confirmation. DCI Bob's smile widens. The look on his face tells me he's convinced he's just nailed the case.

'It was near the start of our relationship,' Rory confirms. 'She'd been in bits and pieces, but nothing worth shouting about. I sent her this before she went for an audition for a recurring character in a drama. ITV I think it was. Anyway, the inscription was to show her that I believed in her.'

Bob looks thoroughly unconvinced by the story though I feel a twinge of sympathy and, for the first time since I sat down opposite the supposed killer, a hint of doubt.

'Why did you turn up at your fiancée's mother's house?' DCI Bob asks, once Rory has had time to compose himself.

'Fiancée,' Rory repeats in a growl. 'You make it sound like she is still around. She was murdered if you remember.'

His lawyer pats his arm and gives him a reassuring nod.

'OK, why did you turn up at Anna's mother's house? he says.

'I had a few jobs that I'd started that I needed to finish. Like I said, for a few days I couldn't bring myself to visit her again, but I always fully intended to come back and finish them for her.'

'And you think turning up late last night was the most appropriate time?'

He shrugs his shoulders. 'I'm heading back down to London tomorrow and thought that if I could sleep there, get up early and have a full day at her house, I could get all the jobs finished up.'

'And an alibi, perhaps?' DCI Bob says with a hint of a grin. Rory's eyes narrow in confusion and his lawyer sits forward in his chair. 'You know who Ed Bennett is, don't you?' Bob continues.

'He's the author, isn't he? I've met him once or twice.'

'Didn't like him, did you?' Bob asks.

Rory doesn't rise to the bait, his lips remain firmly shut.

'So you think he might recognise you?'

'I think he might. He was there the night I confronted Reuben at the book shop. I also met him on the set of a film many years ago. Then again, I didn't recognise him on the CCTV footage you showed me, the first time I came here,' he says to me.

'Do you know that he has recently gone missing? Last night, actually. DI Piper here was on the phone to him as he was kidnapped. He seemed to know his kidnapper...' Bob trails off and lets silence fill the room.

'What are you trying to get at here?' the lawyer asks calmly.

'What I'm suggesting,' counters Bob, 'is that Mr Knox abducted Ed Bennett, dumped the body somewhere and then turned up at Anna's house in the hope of an alibi.'

'And what evidence do you have?'

'We're working on that,' says Bob. 'Now, let's move on to the evidence we do have at hand. We've checked the hammer in the toolbox you had with you when you reappeared. It's clean. So you're in the clear there. This however...' he trails off, lifting a laptop onto the table and opening the lid which awakens the screen.

Bob presses a few buttons and the video of Reuben's hanging appears. Whilst Rory and his lawyer take in what is happening on the screen, I keep my focus on Rory's face. He looks uneasy at the sight of Reuben's bloodied visage and seems confused as to why he is being made to watch this.

The lawyer's face is frozen in concentration, his keen eyes taking in every second of the footage. When Rory's voice emanates from the laptop, their facial expressions change. Rory's head jerks back and his eyes widen in shock at the sound of his own voice. The lawyer is looking at his client out of the corners of his eyes, knowing his job just got that little bit harder.

Rory opens his mouth to speak but the lawyer wags a finger, indicating for him to hold his tongue. I expect the lawyer to sound panicked, but when he speaks after pausing the laptop, his voice is even, measured.

'I assume you think this proves something?' he asks.

'It's *his* voice,' Bob replies, pointing at Rory.

The lawyer shakes his head. 'It's a voice that sounds like my client's. However, anyone could put on an accent and edit it into a video. This proves nothing.'

DCI Bob reaches across and presses play on the video again. Reuben's pleas fill the room and when the box he's standing on is kicked from underneath him, Bob pauses the video again.

'Look at the boot,' Bob says to Rory. 'Look familiar?'

Bob reaches below the table and sets a pair of boots on the table.

'My mother, God rest her soul, always used to say it was bad luck to put shoes on a table, and I guess for you,' he glances at Rory, 'it is.'

A muscle in Rory's jaw twitches, but he remains silent.

'The boots are a match; we had our tech team look at them last night. Now, these boots were used to kick away the box that was supporting poor Reuben, the prints were also found in some mud near the body of Jason Krist, who Rory also didn't see eye to eye with, and on Anna's face. If you look carefully at the video,' Bob zooms in on the boot, 'the scuffs on the heel and on the inside toe are identical.'

When I look from the boot to Rory, I notice that he has tears streaming down his face.

'Hit a nerve, have we?' chides Bob.

Rory doesn't fight back; it looks like the will to live has left him. 'I didn't kill anyone,' he mutters, the words coming out thick with emotion.

'That's where our opinions differ. I think you killed your fiancée when you found out who she was meeting at the bar. You've admitted to seeing the photograph of them online, and would have had plenty of time to get back from Bradford. Then, you went on a calculated killing spree, wiping out anyone connected with her and her affair.'

Rory is shaking his head vehemently, though Bob takes no notice.

'We are combing Ed's house now for the slightest trace of evidence to put you at the scene. I think that will do for now,' DCI Bob says, and halts the recording. 'Someone will be here soon to escort you back to your cell.'

I TAKE A SWIG from my bottle of water and set it back on Bob's desk. Before the interview, I was convinced of Rory's guilt. Now, I'm not so sure. The surprise on his face when he heard his voice looked genuine, and his tears at the end seemed more out of sheer sadness for Anna than for himself and his impending incarceration.

Bob looks like the cat that got the cream; he is fully convinced of Rory's guilt and is currently on the phone to Martin, informing him of the incoming manpower to help at Ed's house.

He makes it very clear to the head of the forensic team that the window is closing and we need this conviction. He sets down the phone and flashes a smile.

'I'm not sure he's our man,' I say and I notice Bob's smile falters slightly.

'I know we don't have enough to convict him, yet, but soon we will. All the evidence is piling up against him. We just need to put him at the scene. We're on the home stretch. You've done a great job on this, Erika. A fucking great job.'

His fingers pull at the hairs of his goatee and suddenly he looks awkward.

'Look, I've been thinking. The toll this case is taking on you must be enormous, especially with the personal threats and the,' he hesitates for a beat, 'the location of Reuben's murder. I'm giving you the weekend off to get your head straight.'

I'm about to argue that that is the last thing I need, especially at this stage of the investigation, but he ploughs on.

'The first case back after time off is never easy, especially after what you've been through.'

'Because of you,' I snap, taking him by surprise. 'A year ago, you valued catching that fucking drugged up prick over my safety. Sending me into that mill almost cost me my life, and that's on you. Now, you're worried that I am not coping after receiving a threatening text message from someone, you believe, we have in custody. So don't give me that shit about being worried about me.'

'You know how I feel about that. I think about that decision every day of my fucking life,' he says, his voice rising. 'I almost killed you, and I would have had to live with that. I care about you, you know I do. And I just want to do what's best for you. I think a few days out of this place will be for the best.'

'Is that an order?'

I repeat the words I'd said into the radio a year ago, whilst outside the mill. That day, they were asked shakily as the adrenaline began to course through my body. Today, every syllable drips with venom. He doesn't answer.

I can feel the tears waiting to throw themselves down my face and every sinew in my body wants to protest, to scream, though I know it will be in vain.

Instead, I march out of the room before he can see my tears and make my way to the toilet. Once I reach the cubicle, I collapse onto the cold plastic seat and sob. How can he take me off the case now? At the most critical point? Does he think that I'm weak? That I can't do my job properly anymore? I dab my eyes with toilet paper and once the tears have subsided, I unlock the door and walk to the sink.

Luckily, I didn't put mascara on this morning so my face isn't as messy as it could have been. I look gaunt and my skin looks pale and waxy under the fluorescent strip lighting. I give myself a shake, splash some cold water on my face and leave the toilet, taking the long way round to the stairs so that I don't have to walk past Bob's office again.

The low, winter sun is shining and I have to squint as I leave the station. I pull my phone out of my pocket and find Tom's name in my dialled calls list. I press his name and put the phone to my ear. It rings for a time but he doesn't answer and I can feel the tears threatening to spill again. I know he is not supposed to be back until tomorrow, and I can't imagine the stress he is dealing with, but I just want to hear his voice.

I get into my car and throw my bag onto the passenger seat. DCI Bob may have sent me on a little holiday, but that doesn't mean I have to stop working.

In fact, I fully intend to use this time to prove to DCI Bob that Rory is not our killer, and that whoever *is* guilty is very much still on the loose. I may not be on the case anymore, but I'm determined to get the right guy.

29

MY ALARM RINGS AND I sit bolt upright in bed. In an effort to prevent me from pressing snooze and lazing about, the phone is connected to a charger on the opposite side of the room, forcing me to get out of bed and retrieve it.

As I turn the alarm off, yesterday's conversation with DCI Bob runs through my mind and I realise that I have nowhere to be. I slip the phone into my pyjama pocket and clamber back into the bed, rejoicing as the warmth envelops me once more.

I roll over and close my eyes, though my brain has whirred into motion, and once it starts there is no stopping it. I linger on the reason I am free to lie about and relax; it's a 'reward' for doing my job. A reward. *No-one else is enjoying a few days off for doing the job they are paid to do; he thinks you're weak*, chirps the devil on my shoulder.

Whatever Bob's reasons, I don't like it. I don't like this freedom, especially when my time and energy could be harnessed elsewhere. Particularly, so close to the conclusion of the case.

I check my phone again and note that there is no communication from the station. Either they are treating me with a *cordon sanitaire* or, more likely, there hasn't been any progress made.

I open my news app and am shocked to see DCI Bob's face attached to the first story. I press on the article and find out that DCI Bob has released details of an arrest. It obviously refers to Rory, though my boss hasn't mentioned his name, instead insisting that *The Blood Ice Killer* has been caught.

Having not heard anything from the station, I presume that this is a strategy to get the press off his back. It's a risky one, as, if nothing happens soon, they'll have to release Rory. There simply isn't enough evidence to charge him and if they are forced to let him go, DCI Bob will be under all sorts of scrutiny.

I make a vow that I will have a productive day. But first, a phone call I should've made a week ago.

Dad sounds like he is trying to put on a brave face and hold it together, though he is failing miserably. The despair and deep-rooted sadness of my mum's death last year is obvious in every word he utters.

He asks about my work and I tell him it is going well, though I neglect to tell him about my 'holiday'. We discuss his ongoing DIY projects and speculate on the sex of Sarah's baby, the prospect of becoming a grandfather seemingly a light at the end of the tunnel for him.

Before hanging up, I promise that I will visit tomorrow and he sounds cheered by this. When I finish the call, I lie back on the bed and sob. Dad's now solitary life has really hit me between the eyes and I feel bad that I have prioritised the case over the needs of my family. Once I've sat up and wiped the tears off my face, I vow to make some changes.

I check Twitter and, even though news of Reuben Amaro's death was trending for a few days, already it seems people have moved on. There is no mention yet of Ed's disappearance, though I imagine DCI Bob is already busy drafting a speech for another press conference scheduled for later in the day.

I check Ed's Twitter page and note that he barely uses it. The most recent post is from last year, and is a RT from a blogger praising his latest work. He didn't bother replying.

I open my phonebook and consider calling Bob, to check in and see if there is anything I can do, remotely. I hover over his name but ultimately decide against it. I can hear his dismissive tone and his refusal to divulge anything.

Instead, I navigate to Martin's number and press on it. It takes a nanosecond to realise that it is a bad idea and I press the red button before the call has a chance to connect. If Martin knows I'm supposed to be taking time off, he'll be straight to Bob to let him know I'm meddling. He is a stickler for the rules.

Frustrated, I throw my phone onto the Sherlock chair where it lands with a small bounce and a dull thud.

I take a slurp from the still-hot coffee cup and open the lid of my laptop. Though the case against him is pretty good, the feeling that Rory is innocent in all of this still niggles at me.

I log in to the police database and access the file containing all the information related to this case. I re-read the details of Anna's death; the actual killing, the book page, the removed, though never recovered, tongue. Someone who followed the words in *The Threat* as gospel. Finally, I scan over the photos but there is no new information to be collected.

I open the file containing the material concerning Jay's murder. As I read, a statement from John, the forensic pathologist, jumps out at me. The trauma to the head must've been delivered by someone tall. We know this from the position of the blows. However, the number of blows it took to kill Jay suggest a weakness in the attacker. This corroborates what Ben told DCI Bob during his interview about hearing Jay's attacker cough as he walked away.

I grab my phone from the seat and find John's number. I call him and pray that he is alone when he answers. Luckily, God has listened.

'Erika, how are you?' he says. He sounds tired. I tell him that I am well and move swiftly onto business.

'I was just wondering if you'd finished Reuben's post-mortem yet?'

'Not long ago, actually. I haven't written the report yet,' he says, apologetically.

'Don't worry about it,' I reply. 'I'm just exploring an avenue with regards to his death at the minute, and was wondering if there was anything odd about your findings?'

'Not really,' he says, much to my disappointment. 'The killing is very much in keeping with the others; unbelievable violence and a nasty end.'

He assures me that as soon as he completes the report, it will be on my desk. I thank him and hang up. *Hmm, nothing new gleaned there.*

I pull up the photographs from Ed's house. The downstairs rooms are exactly as I remember them; the door kicked off its hinges and lying on its side, the streak of blood on the frame. I'm reminded of that crappy action film Tom had chosen the night before he left for home. I think back to the house in the opening scene with the perfectly distributed shards of glass and the broken television. I look at the pictures on my laptop screen again. Am I really looking at a crime scene or simply what *appears* to be a crime scene?

I study each picture intently. Everything seems a little too... set up. With fresh eyes, the door perfectly balanced on its side takes on more importance. The smashed-up living room, the small dots of blood splattered on the stairs. It all looks a little too perfect, too organised.

Once I've exhausted the photographs of downstairs, I start on the upstairs. I study his bedroom, though I can't see anything of importance. Next, the bathroom. My eyes are drawn to the bathroom cabinet straight away and I remember the tablet packet I took a picture of on my phone.

I grab the phone again and open the picture album, scrolling to find the one I need. Checking the image, I type the name of the medication into Google. I choose the first website and discover that this tablet is prescribed to treat nausea, potentially caused by drugs associated with the treatment of cancer. I click on a few more to verify this information and it seems to be true.

So Ed has cancer? And then the penny drops. It all makes sense; the tablets, the mannequin head; presumably used to hold his wig. The man with the bald head hobbling away from the alley containing Jay's bludgeoned body. I recall how his movements seemed hampered when we first visited him and remember his coughing fit which he had passed off as a simple cold. It was him all along.

Another photograph, a few along from the tablets catches my eye. The dedication in the card to his mother, written in block capitals. I scroll through my camera roll until I come to the graffiti left behind at Jay's crime scene and study the letters. There are certain similarities; the vertical stroke of the letter T that extends past the horizontal, reminiscent of a cross and the c that is formed by two diagonal lines. It's almost definitely his writing.

I think of the card found in Anna's bedroom; the looping, artistically formed letters. Rory was telling the truth when he said he had sent it for all the right reasons.

My mind springs to Reuben's murder. Reuben probably thought they were making some sort of publicity video for the upcoming film, which would've been in both Ed's and his interests.

I picture Reuben turning up at the warehouse, imagining a fun day with his friend, and the horror he must've felt when he realised exactly what was happening. How, having slipped the noose around his neck, he had just signed his own death warrant. The stinging comprehension that he was about to be murdered by his best friend.

I push the laptop away and retrieve a notebook from a drawer on the kitchen cabinet. I scrawl the names of the victims and any motive he would've had for killing them. Jay is the simplest to pin down; being thrown off the film set of your own book must be pretty embarrassing. He had mentioned about Jay screwing him over with a contract too. However, I can't think of a reason why he would've killed Anna so brutally or what would have driven him to murder his best friend, Reuben.

I pull the laptop towards me again and open up the video of Reuben's hanging. I skip the video forward until the killer's voice appears. I half expect the voice to have changed to Ed's, but what it booms out of the laptop speakers, it is unmistakably Rory's.

Frustrated, I push myself away from the table and walk to the counter to pour myself a glass of water. As I set my glass down, I notice my earphones sitting near the fruit bowl. I spend a few minutes untangling them before plugging them into a port on the side of the laptop.

I slip them into my ears and press play on the video again. The sounds in the video are rendered clearer by the earphones, and I close my eyes to help focus further on the audio.

As Rory's speaks, I can feel my body tense. As he is about to finish his sentence, questioning Reuben about supposedly killing Anna, I hear a sound I hadn't heard before. It takes me by surprise and I don't fully register the content.

I rewind the video again and press play, straining my ears to make sure I'm ready. As Rory finishes his question, the sound quickly becomes clear. A gasp. A collective gasp from a room full of book lovers that transports me back to The Book Club on the night of Ed and Reuben's joint event.

At that point, there was no way of him knowing that Rory would be bursting in and publicly accusing Reuben of murder. Reuben and he were simply recording a podcast for fans who couldn't make the events.

He must've been thanking whatever god he believes in for such an opportunity, and for the role he played in diffusing the tension; coming out the good guy.

This is the final piece of the puzzle. I find Martin's number and hit the green button.

'Hello?' he says, sounding confused.

The noise in the background tells me that he and his team are still working away at Ed's house.

'Hi, how's it going?'

'OK, aren't you supposed to be resting?' he asks. I wonder what sort of message DCI Bob has given to the rest of the team. Are they supposed to ignore me as a tactic to pressure me into making sure I'm following Bob's advice?

'I am, I just have a quick question. You know the fingerprint you found on the page recovered from Jay's murder scene, did you get a match?'

Martin tells me that there was no match on the IDENT1 system for that fingerprint, though it has now been logged in case of a match down the line.

I tell him that I am 99% certain that it is Ed's fingerprint and to test it against his prints found in his house as soon as he can. He confirms that he will and hangs up. Next, I dial Liam.

'Aren't you on holiday?' he teases. 'What can I do for you?

'Can't a friend simply call a friend to say hello?' I ask in reply.

'Is that what is happening here?'

He sounds suspicious, like he already knows that this is not what is happening here.

'Well, no,' I admit, 'I have a theory. I think Rory is innocent.'

'Give me a minute,' he says. I hear a door close and the background noise dies down. 'Ok, go.'

I tell him every detail of my research and the evidence I've collected. He remains silent throughout and when I finish, he tells me that there has been no new evidence found to incriminate Rory overnight and that DCI Bob is fuming.

He agrees that my theory has legs and that I should call Bob and run it by him. I tell him I will, though I have no intention of doing that just yet.

As he is about to go, he asks if I've heard from Tom, as he was supposed to be in work this afternoon but hasn't turned up and that no-one can get in touch with him.

I suggest that maybe he has been delayed leaving his parent's place and that I will try.

I hang up and dial Tom's number. It doesn't ring for long before the call connects and Tom answers with a grunt. It sounds like I have woken him up.

'Tom, are you OK?'

He grunts again and I remember that he didn't answer my call yesterday and I wonder if I have done something to annoy him.

'Have you left Oxford yet? Liam says you haven't made it to work today.'

Much to my annoyance, there is still no answer. I decide to tell him what I have been working on, to see if the news will elicit a response.

'I think Ed is the killer.'

'Took you long enough,' a voice says, though the voice does not belong to Tom.

It belongs to Ed.

'Don't tell anyone about this phone call, and come straight here. You know where to find me. If you tell anyone about this, your boyfriend dies,' he snarls, before the line goes dead.

30

WHEN I LEFT THE HOUSE, I was certain that I was making the right decision in coming to meet Ed. Now, as I near the meeting point, I can't help but feel I am walking into the lion's den. I've adhered to his demand of keeping quiet about the phone call and coming alone, though I've almost turned back a number of times. The thought of Tom keeps me going. I don't even know for certain that he is still alive, but I have to believe he is.

My blood runs cold as I approach my destination. The part of the suburb in the south of the city feels as though it has been forgotten, the crumbling buildings and the high-rise tower blocks covered in graffiti are testament to the fact.

As I indicate onto an unlit lane, the warehouse looms in front of me, blotting out the stars. I slow the car and crawl up the pock-marked road, attempting to keep my approach as quiet as possible.

The sight of the warehouse turns my stomach and elicits a phantom pain in my torso as I imagine the steel blade slipping into it. It takes all my willpower not to turn the car around.

Instead, my grip tightens on the steering wheel and I drive through the gates of the abandoned warehouse, bringing the car to a stop.

Even though I have taken care not to draw attention to my arrival, I'm sure I am being watched. Of course I am. I scan the row of broken windows near the top of the building, though I can't make out any shapes there.

I pull my gun from its holster, lower it to my side and open the car door, taking care to close it quietly. I edge along the wall of the building towards the space where a door should be.

Memories from last year flood my mind; the darkness that enveloped me as I entered the silent space, the cold concrete below my feet. The machine gun rhythm of my heart.

Already, I know that tonight is going to be different. I'm in a small entranceway, a sort of antechamber that serves the main room. It smells of damp and is littered with broken glass which crunches beneath my feet. Unruly weeds have begun to populate the area.

I walk through them and push my back against the archway which links this room with the open space beyond. A low humming sound interrupts the landscape of silence, though the source is unknown. I crane my neck around the doorway and sneak a peek into the mill.

It is split into two levels; the ground floor is bare, showing no evidence of the hard graft that would've been characteristic of the room in years gone by. The concrete floor seems to emanate coldness and lumps of the hard material have been knocked out leaving small potholes, a side effect of the removal of the machinery that once dominated the place.

The first floor is reached by a spiral staircase, the walkways above are rusted and look like they could give way at any moment. A set of spotlights bathe the room in a warm glow and are powered by a small generator. I realise now that that is where the humming noise is coming from. It lends the warehouse a film-set quality.

I'm not even sure Ed is here. There was no sign of another vehicle out front. This could all be an elaborate ruse, getting me here so that he can commit another atrocity somewhere else.

In the middle of the vast expanse of space is Tom.

He sits on a wooden chair, his arms bound behind him with thick, blue rope. His head has lolled forward, his chin resting on his chest. I pull my head back round the corner and try to formulate a plan.

The room has no places to hide; if I try and get directly to Tom, I'll be a moving target. If I stay here and wait for Ed to make the first move, I could be here all night.

I decide that Tom's safety is paramount. I glance out one more time, before launching myself out of the doorway and sprinting towards Tom. I half expect to be taken down in a haze of bullets, though none are forthcoming and I reach Tom safely, who I now realise is sitting in the exact spot where Reuben's life was ended.

I take Tom's head in my hands and stroke his cheeks, his stubble rough against my fingertips. I check for a pulse and find one easily. Apart from being unconscious and having a slightly swollen, bruised eye, he doesn't seem to be badly hurt.

'Tom, wake up,' I plead, my voice echoing around the vast space. 'He's going to kill us both.'

'Bingo!' a voice shouts, from the top of the steps.

I instinctively raise my gun, though I can't see the source of the noise.

'Now,' he continues from his vantage point, 'we both know that you having a gun is not going to work. So, slowly, and I do mean slowly, put the safety on and throw it towards the bottom of the steps. Then get down on your knees.'

I rack my brains for another option, though my train of thought is quickly interrupted by a gunshot aimed close to Tom's head. It's a threat, but enough of one to remind me that he is capable of murder.

The bullet causes broken glass to cascade from one of the windows behind me.

'Do it, now!' he bellows, before succumbing to a coughing fit.

I follow his instructions and toss my only weapon in the direction of the steps. It bounces off the bottom step and the jarring sound of metal on metal fills the room. I get on my knees and put my hands behind my head.

Footsteps sound on the steps. His feet appear, followed by the rest of his body. Finally, I am staring Ed in the face.

He is thinner than last time we met, his skin seemingly retreating into his body as his bones venture in the opposite direction. His dark wig, which is slightly askew, accentuates the paleness of his skin. He points his own gun at me with a shaking hand.

'How nice of you to join us,' he jeers. He steps onto the cold floor and takes small steps towards me, gun still raised.

'Why here?' I ask him.

He smiles an ugly smile.

'Well, my first two kills were exactly as I'd written them; the blonde bombshell actress splayed across the ice, throat slit and the important business man, film producer Jay, clubbed to death with a hammer. And then you came a-calling,' he says, 'and I knew where I was going to kill my best friend. You see, I recognised you straight away, the brave police officer who almost died in the derelict warehouse. I knew that if you saw the video of Reuben,' he mimics a noose tightening around his neck, 'you'd know exactly where to find his body and we'd all end up here.'

He sits down on the bottom step and pulls his wig off. He reaches into his jacket pocket and pulls out a handkerchief. He coughs into it and when he pulls it away from his mouth, there are spots of blood staining it.

'So you've got cancer? And I presume that's why you've done all this? Some sense of justice against the world?' I goad him.

A flash of anger crosses his face but when he speaks again, his voice is considered.

'Not at all,' he replies. 'When I got my terminal diagnosis, I felt neither anger or panic, I felt nothing. I knew it was coming, accepted it and thought I'd just fade away. But then I got reading about legacies and spent a lot of time thinking about mine. What am I going to leave to the world when I go?'

With some effort, he hauls himself up from the step and rubs the barrel of the gun against his bald head. It looks rehearsed and feels insincere, like he is playing a character he has written.

'I concluded that all I would be leaving behind were my stories. And that's when I began to form the idea for my killing spree. You see, even though my novels are well known, the bastardised film version of *Blood Ice* is much more famous. And that's what I will forever be remembered for; sub-standard films.'

He begins to pace.

'So I thought by killing the people involved in them; Anna, Jay, Reuben and finally myself, the limelight would fall back on me and my books. People will hate me but everyone will want to know why I did it. That's the brilliance of the human mind; we are fascinated by what we can't understand. So, when the fourth book in the *Threat* series, a crime book with an autobiographical slant, is released, posthumously, it'll fly off the shelves and my infamy will be confirmed.'

The speech sounds prepared and is delivered with more than a hint of theatrical nuance. He walks towards me, his gun still trained on my head.

'Throw in a couple of dead cops and we have ourselves the perfect finale. I'll be remembered forever.'

'Why dress as a homeless man?' I ask, in an attempt to buy some time.

He barks a laugh that echoes around the room.

'Ah, my finest idea. You see, when I first came up with the idea, I only planned on the one death. It was always going to be the one on the rink, but I never thought it would be Anna. That was just a stroke of fortune. I thought leaving the page at the scene would lead the police to me, and if it didn't, I was going to admit to the death via a social media post scheduled for when I'd died. But then I got a taste for it, it became a bit of a game, seeing how far I could go. Manchester is, sadly, full of homeless people and I thought that if I could fade into the group, my identity could remain hidden for long enough to get us to this point.'

'You said you never planned on killing Anna. But you did. How did you get to her?'

'Pure chance,' he admits. 'When I formed my plan, I thought any blonde would do. I could get chatting to one in a bar, drug her and go through with my little scheme. But social media came through for me.'

The confusion must show on my face.

'She put a picture on Instagram. Some inane photograph of a smoothie with the hashtag GoodToBeHome. Why people feel the need to share every little detail of their life is beyond me. Anyway, I know the shop and to be fair to her, they do make fantastic smoothies. It was then I figured that she was up north. When we got to the bar, Reuben ordered some drinks and went to the toilet but left his phone on the table. I sent her a message from Reuben's phone, inviting her down to Limas, and deleted the evidence. The only thing that could screw it all up was if she asked him why he had texted her. Thankfully, British-ness prevailed and she engaged in polite chit-chat long enough for me to slip some Rohypnol into her drink.'

'But why her?' I ask. 'She didn't do anything wrong.'

'I agree,' he replies. 'But if I'd used some local girl, the news would've stayed local. Anna was my ticket to international exposure. People care so much more about famous people because they think they know them. Even the locals don't care that much if one of their own has been killed. They're simply a name on the front of a newspaper for a day, then they are history. Forgotten about.'

'And when you staged your kidnapping, was that to get the press talking too?'

'Bang on,' he says. 'But it didn't work, because you didn't release the details to the media. I thought there would be a hastily arranged press conference with my face plastered all over it. The poor author next to die unless the public have any information on his whereabouts. Then, when I saw that Rory had been arrested, I knew the time had come to blow the story open and cement my name into history.'

He glances past me at the unmoving body in the chair.

'Speaking of which,' he says. 'Let's kill your boyfriend.'

He takes a couple of steps towards Tom and I try to reason with him, to assure him that his final days can be made pain-free and peaceful. That he doesn't need to kill anyone else.

A well-placed kick to my side knocks the wind out of me and leaves me gasping for air.

'You're wrong,' he shouts, 'if I don't kill both of you, my final days will be spent in a jail cell. That isn't happening. No, we're all going to die here tonight. Starting with him,' he says, pointing the gun at Tom.

He steps past me and whilst his attention is on Tom, I feel around on the floor behind me for anything I could use as a weapon, though all I can locate is a rusted bolt. As Ed raises the gun to Tom's head, I throw the bolt towards the area behind them.

The resulting clang of bolt meeting floor causes Ed to momentarily divert his attention from Tom, and that moment is all I need. I push myself off the floor and, leading with my shoulder, barge into his side, sending us both sprawling onto the floor. The gun tumbles across the ground and out of reach.

I position myself on top of him, straddling his chest whilst trying to control his flailing, emaciated arms. I can feel his rib cage rising and falling with the effort of trying to overturn me.

Despite having a terminal illness, his strength is impressive. His long limbs are difficult to control and when he catches my side with a well-placed punch, I struggle to remain on top.

Another punch strikes me and I fall off him and onto the floor, the cold creeping up my back. My discomfort intensifies as Ed places himself on my chest. He holds each of my arms to the ground with his knees and grins in my face as his hand tightens around my throat.

I kick my legs and try to swivel my torso with all the energy I can muster, though it isn't enough to shift him. Coloured spots start to appear in my vision and I think of my dad.

Tears stream down my face as I imagine him opening the door tomorrow, expecting to see me but being greeted instead by a pair of uniformed police officers, bearing news no parent should ever have to face.

As his grip tightens, I feel my body give up and I begin to drift towards the welcoming darkness.

A HUGE CRASH ECHOES around the room and the grip on my throat relaxes slightly. Gulping in as much air as possible, I turn my head and see Tom getting to his feet with Ed's discarded gun in his hand, the wooden chair splintered into several pieces.

Ed swears loudly and uses a reserve of strength to hoist me off the ground. He holds me tight to his chest with one long arm, his hand grasping my stomach; the other brandishes a shard of glass which glints in the light. The two men engage in a Mexican standoff, sizing each other up.

'Put the gun down,' Ed yells. His breathing has become strained and I can feel his ribs digging into my back.

'Let her go,' Tom replies, his tone calm. He's looking past me and into the eyes of my captor.

'Put the fucking gun down,' he shouts, louder this time. When Tom doesn't immediately comply, Ed brings the sharp fragment of glass to my face and drags it across my cheek. The glass easily tears the skin under my eye and leaves a deep, ragged gash from which blood cascades down my face. As he pulls the shard away, a bloodcurdling scream escapes my lips.

'If I have to ask you one more time, it's her throat next,' he hisses, and I can feel the glass graze the side of my neck. 'Now, for the last time, put the fucking gun down.'

He utters each syllable slowly, as if he is talking to someone who doesn't speak the same language. The hand on my stomach is shaking violently now and I worry about his state of mind.

Tom's eyes meet mine.

'Don't!' I shout at him. 'Whatever you do, he'll kill us both!'

I can feel the blood enter my mouth and I gag, the metallic tang almost making me vomit.

'Erika, I'm sorry,' he says.

At the sight of him giving in, all the fight left in my body leaves. I relax against Ed's frame, ready to have my throat torn open, to receive my fate. Tom bends down slowly, the gun extended in front of him with one hand raised in a sign of submission. Ed's body relaxes slightly and then Tom pulls the trigger.

The noise of the gunshot explodes through my ears and into my brain, rendering me incapacitated.

A pleasant warmth spreads though the top of my leg and it takes me a moment to realise that it must be blood. Ed's grip around my torso loosens though I'm still dragged to the floor, landing on top of him. My hand immediately jumps to my thigh, searching for the injury that is causing the blood loss. Though unable to find a bullet wound, my hand comes away slick with blood.

I can feel myself being pulled from Ed's slack grip and as I'm delivered to a standing position, I brace myself for the pain to really hit. It doesn't come.

After a minute of disorientation, the scene reveals itself; Ed is still lying on the ground, screaming in pain and clutching his leg whilst Tom has removed the bullets from the gun and made it safe, content that the threat to life has been subdued.

As I pull my phone out to call the ambulance, Tom drops to his knees and attempts to stem the blood flow from Ed's leg by tearing a strip of material from the sleeve of his t-shirt and using it as a form of tourniquet.

Once Tom is convinced that the first-aid he has provided to Ed is enough to keep him alive until the ambulance arrives, he turns him onto his back and I cuff his skeletal wrists.

Tom wraps me in his arms and we sink to the floor, to the soundtrack of sirens in the distance.

I WINCE AS THE anaesthetic begins to wear off and I can feel the pain flare in the area under my eye. The doctor has closed the gash with a number of stitches and after a thorough assessment, was happy that no lasting damage has been done to my throat by Ed's vice-like grip.

Whilst waiting for the doctor to finish giving Tom the once over, I open the email Angela has sent through and re-watch the CCTV footage of Ed waiting at the bus stop outside Limas. Once the bus arrives, he steps on and when the bus leaves the frame, so does he. I open up the new file that Angela has managed to source at short notice. It is CCTV footage from the bus stop approximately 300 metres along the road.

Ed can clearly be seen getting off the bus and disappearing into an alleyway between a gastro-pub called The Brewhouse and a Sainsbury's local.

After a few minutes, Ed re-appears, though this time disguised as the homeless man who later that night murdered Anna so viciously. He is now carrying a bigger bag, presumably filled with his murder implements. I close the file and shake my head at the sheer audacity of his actions.

As I slip my phone back into my pocket, DCI Bob eases himself into the seat beside me.

'How's the patient?' he asks.

'He'll live,' I respond, my tone making it clear that I'm still pissed off with him.

'The results from the prints on Ed's door frame came back. They are a match for the prints found on the page at the second murder. There's no denying now that Ed is the killer.'

'Good,' I reply. Frosty.

He takes off his glasses and rubs each lens with his tie before replacing them on his nose.

'Look, I know you're not happy but I stand by what I did,' he sighs, 'I was doing the right thing for you and I'd do the same again. I've learned from my fuck-up last year.'

I realise that this is probably the closest I'm going to get to an apology and my resolve is broken. Maybe he was thinking of my wellbeing all along and I was simply too proud or paranoid to see it from his point of view. I give his shoulder a squeeze and he gives me a small smile.

'Shall we go and see our man?' he asks, before getting to his feet.

We walk side by side towards intensive care, the soles of DCI Bob's shoes squeak on the recently buffed floor, where Ed is currently being treated for the gunshot wound to his leg.

Outside his room is a uniformed officer, making sure no-one comes or goes. We relieve him of his duty and he looks pleased to have a break. He makes his way down the corridor towards the cafeteria.

When we enter the room, a young doctor is completing some final checks and when the he is done, Ed offers his hand into which the doctor inserts a drip. Though he is following the doctor's orders, he is staring, unblinking, at us.

His wig has been removed and the white walls make his skin appear paler than ever. The doctor makes sure Ed does not need any more pain relief before leaving the room.

'Sorry about that,' he sneers, motioning to the cut under my eye with his untethered hand. Ignoring him, I sit in the uncomfortable, plastic chair in the corner of the room, whilst DCI Bob leans against the window.

I read him his charges and, all the while, he looks thoroughly pleased with himself.

Anna Symons' murder on Saturday the first of December.

He nods his head.

Jason Krist's murder on Wednesday the fifth of December.

This one elicits a smile.

Reuben Amaro's murder sometime between Thursday the sixth of December and Sunday the ninth of December.

An even wider smile this time.

Finally, the abduction and attempted murder of Thomas Calder and the attempted murder of myself, Erika Piper.

When I finish talking, he laughs.

'Do you understand what I've just said to you?' I ask.

He looks at me like I have just read him the menu for tomorrow's meals.

'Perfectly,' he smiles.

'The end of *The Blood Ice Killer*,' says DCI Bob.

Ed barks a hollow laugh.

'The fucking irony is hilarious. The fact I was doing all of this to take the attention away from the film and bring it back to the books, and that's the title they give me. I was hoping for something like *The Threat*. Sounds a bit like a superhero, doesn't it?'

I can see DCI Bob shaking his head out of the corner of my eye. I ignore Ed's attempt at joviality and instead pull my notebook out of my pocket.

'Since we're here, would you mind clearing up a few things?' I say, to which he inclines his head.

'Why did you try to frame Rory?'

He laughs. 'That was my insurance policy. By then, I'd got a taste for killing. I thought that if he went down for the deaths, I could carry on for a while before you lot realised your mistake. It was also a massive slice of luck that he made such a scene whilst we were recording the podcast! It would've felt amateur not to play with him.'

'When you were crying at the premiere, were you acting for my benefit?'

'Believe it or not, no,' he says, becoming slightly sombre. 'I still have a heart, and seeing what I'd done, I felt something close to remorse. But then, he had butchered the film adaptations of my books, so in the end, it felt justified.'

Bob walks around the bed and loiters near the door.

'Son,' he says, 'isn't the legacy you are leaving behind worse than a few naff films?'

'Let me put it this way,' Ed replies. 'Imagine you aren't a policeman, you're just a member of the public. You've never heard of me. Someone tells you they watched a shit film and that is based on a book. Are you going to read the book?'

DCI Bob shakes his head.

'Now imagine someone tells you that this set of books was written by a terminally ill man who became a serial killer. Would you read them then?'

'I'd certainly be more inclined to,' he admits.

'And that is my point. People are fascinated by death. We slow down when we drive past car crashes to assess the damage, to try and get a little glimpse of death, to revel in someone's worst, possibly final, moment. We love death because we do not understand it. And when I am gone, which will be reasonably soon, the book sales will soar. And that's my legacy. For good or for bad, at least they'll remember me.'

I've heard enough. I push myself out of the chair and head for the door, DCI Bob in my wake.

'See you in court,' I say, over my shoulder.

The noise that escapes his mouth is a mixture of laughter and coughing.

'The next time you see me will be in Hell.'

EPILOGUE

EIGHT WEEKS LATER

I CHECK MY WATCH. It's 7:27 p.m. We don't have long.

Guttural screams echo through the corridor, thunderous pleas for help. Tom and I make our way down the hallway at pace, searching for the room we need.

Most of the doors along the corridor are closed, their blinds drawn tight to keep out prying eyes. The room we're looking for is the last on the left. Tom pushes the door slowly and we tiptoe in.

We arrive to a cacophony of noise and the unmistakable stink of lavender. Garish, patterned curtains are drawn around three of the beds but Sarah's remain open.

When she sees us, she lets out a muted greeting so as not to disturb the sleeping baby on her chest. Dad is sitting on a chair at her bedside, completely mesmerised by the new life resting upon his youngest daughter.

As I take in the scene, my heart swells and tears flow freely down my face. Seeing Dad this happy again is something I never thought would happen. I give him a little hug and set the bunch of chrysanthemums on the bedside table.

As I embrace Sarah and whisper my congratulations, the baby stirs and a pair of squinting eyes rake over me.

'Meet Sophie,' trills Sarah, handing me the bundle.

I sit on the edge of the bed, nervous about mishandling the precious cargo. A tiny, wrinkled hand emerges from the blankets and grasps my little finger. I struggle to keep it together, aware that I have never felt a love like this. When I look up, Tom is watching me intently with a huge grin on his face.

Once the nurse has convinced my dad that visiting times are final and non-negotiable, we make our way back down the stairs towards the car park at the rear of the maternity ward.

When Dad has bid us an uncharacteristically teary goodbye, we get into Tom's car and make our way home.

'We could always adopt,' says Tom.

The End

ACKNOWLEDGEMENTS

Firstly, thank YOU! If you are reading this, I assume you have finished the book. I genuinely cannot thank you enough, and really hope that you enjoyed it. There are many people, without whom, you would not be holding this book and to them, I owe a debt of gratitude.

Everyone at Red Dog Press, who have been incredible from the start – always at the end of an e-mail and so enthusiastic about my work. I feel very lucky to be in their safe hands.

Sean, who carefully read my work and pointed out the gaping plot holes as well as how to make the small things better, and who designed the amazing cover (the whole reason I wrote the book in the first place was to have a book cover!) Finally, Richard, for taking care of business.

To all the other wonderfully talented authors in the kennel – thank you for making me feel welcome and for your encouraging words.

To the book square – Danielle, Zoé and Sarah. You have given me so much encouragement and help. I owe Sarah a massive thank you in particular, as she very kindly read each chapter as I wrote it, and gave such lovely feedback. I can honestly say that, without her, I would never have finished the book.

Thank you to all the wonderful authors who agreed to read my book and provide a little quote for me. I approached people I truly respected and whose books I have enjoyed enormously, and was blown away by their kindness.

Thank you to all the incredible book bloggers who accepted me as a newbie reviewer in January 2019 and subsequently supported me as an author. I hope you know that I appreciate how hard you work for no reward, aside from inspiring others to read books you have written about so passionately.

Finally, thank you to my family.

To Sarah, my wife, who does not like crime books but who, for the past year, has let me run ideas past her and never (outwardly) questioned why a psychopath has suddenly appeared in the house.

To Emma and Sophie, my beautiful daughters, for being funny, caring and going to bed in a timely fashion which meant I could crack on with writing this! I hope if you ever read this book, that you enjoy it and that you are as proud of me as I am of you.

If you enjoyed the book, I would appreciate if you left a short review on Amazon, Goodreads and the like. If you didn't like it, maybe keep it to yourself…

ABOUT THE AUTHOR

Originally hailing from the north coast of Northern Ireland and now residing in South Manchester, Chris McDonald has always been a reader.

At primary school, The Hardy Boys inspired his love of adventure before his reading world was opened up by Chuck Palahniuk and the gritty world of crime.

A Wash of Black is his first attempt at writing a book. He came up with the initial idea whilst feeding his baby in the middle of the night, which may not be the best thing to admit, considering the content.

He is a fan of 5-a-side football, heavy metal and dogs.